Salwa Bakr was born in Cairo in 1949. She is the author of seven volumes of short stories (including The *Wiles of Men,* AUC Press, 1997), seven novels (including *The Man from Bashmour,* AUC Press, 2007), and a play. Her work has been translated into nine languages.

Dinah Manisty graduated in Arabic from the School of Oriental and African Studies in 1989 and obtained her Ph.D. in 1993 with a study on the woman's novel in Egypt. She has taught Arabic–English translation at the University of Tunis and served as librarian of general collections at the Institute of Ismaili Studies in London.

D1412533

The Golden Chariot

Salwa Bakr

translated by
Dinah Manisty

The American University in Cairo Press

This edition published in 2008 by
The American University in Cairo Press
113 Sharia Kasr el Aini, Cairo, Egypt
One Rockefeller Plaza, 10th Floor, New York, NY 10020
www.aucpress.com

Copyright © 1991 by Salwa Bakr
First published in Arabic in 1991 as *al-'Araba al-dhahabiya la tas'ad ila-l-sama'*
Protected under the Berne Convention

English translation copyright © 1995 by Dinah Manisty

This edition published by arrangement with the author
First English edition published in 1995 by Garnet Publishing Ltd.

All rights reserved. No part of this publication may be reproduced, stored in a retrieval system, or transmitted in any form or by any means, electronic, mechanical, photocopying, recording, or otherwise, without the prior written permission of the publisher.

Dar el Kutub No. 27023/07
ISBN 978 977 416 179 7

Dar el Kutub Cataloging-in-Publication Data

Bakr, Salwa
The Golden Chariot / Salwa Bakr; translated by Dinah Manisty.—
Cairo: The American University in Cairo Press, 2008
p. cm.
ISBN 977 416 179 3
1. Arabic fiction I. Manisty, Dinah (trans.) II. Title
813

3 4 5 6 7 8 23 22 21 20

Printed in the United States of America

Translator's Note

This novel uses colloquial Arabic to capture the reality of the spoken language for women in Egypt. When transliterating Arabic names and words into English, I have reflected the local pronunciation wherever possible. Thus the traditional Arabic name Rajab has been written as Ragab, following Egyptian phonetics. Umm Ragab means mother of Ragab. The only exception is the word *Hajja*, a title used for a woman who has undertaken the pilgrimage to Mecca, and now commonly used as a form of address for elderly women. This title is used throughout the Islamic world, and I have retained the standard transliteration.

I would like to express my warm thanks to Mukhtar Kraïem of the Arabic Department, Faculty of Human and Social Sciences, University of Tunis, for the valuable advice and support he gave me while translating this novel.

1

Where the River Flows into the Sea

Aziza the Alexandrian woke from her usual midday nap which she took to make up for the long hours she was up during the night, sometimes till dawn. The din of daily life in the women's prison had subsided a little; the laughter mixed with the sound of crying, the habitual quarrels between the inmates over the bathroom, the fights over food and the perpetual shrieks of rebuke from the warders demanding submission to the rules and regulations which governed prison life.

Stretched out on her bed on the floor, she opened her eyes. Through the open window high up in the cell, her gaze rested on the wispy outlines of the trees, now slightly blurred in the fading light. She listened for a few moments to the evening chorus of sparrows which settled on the branches, bidding farewell until the dawn of another day. It was a performance she had listened to at the same time every evening since the first day she came to the prison. The chirping and twittering usually blended with the voices of Sheikh Abdel Baset or Mohamed Rifaat chanting beautiful Qur'anic recitations. It was Hajja

Umm Abdel-Aziz who tuned in the radio to the station which broadcast the Qur'an and placed it on the window ledge of the special block for elderly and disabled prisoners.

Aziza gave a deep sigh when the Sheikh came to the comforting words of the Wise and Almighty: "For you who are punished there is life, O most wise!" She had begun to feel anxious and breathless; the intense humidity of August, which ripened the cotton until it burst open and which made the dates plump and full also brought with it the oppressive weather which dampened her spirit. Sweat smelling of rancid dates trickled down from her neck and from under her arms. She got up and took off her regulation long, prison robe made from white calico and walked across the room. She cupped some water in her hands from the green, plastic bucket in the corner and splashed her face and neck with it. Then she washed under her arms, letting a few drops fall into an old *al-Mizan* ghee can, which was now used for scraps.

She wiped her wet hands over her hair to gather the soft strands which had strayed during sleep from her bun secured with nets and pins. When she had finished she began to walk a little in the big room. One of the windows looked onto the long corridor which led to her cell, and the others, in this block of the prison reserved for disabled, sick and 'special' cases. She tired of walking and went over to the other window, hoping to cool down and lift her spirits with a breath of fresh air; the cold water she had washed herself with had long since dried. All she could see was the high wall topped by barbed wire which separated the women's prison from the men's and a few treetops which were slowly sinking into the darkness. She sighed with irritation and left the window with its thin, iron bars and the bleak outlook which had become engraved on her mind since they had moved her to this cell. She went back to her bed and sat down to begin the solitary evening ritual – which she had followed for many years, where she withdrew into herself and ruminated over her grief and the memories of days past. This was the time she allowed herself to communicate with her lonely soul to relieve it of its pain and torment and shattered hopes.

Aziza lit up a Cleopatra cigarette and inhaled deeply with the pleasure of a heavy smoker, hooked since youth. She gazed at the scattered stars looking down on her from the small chink of clear sky which she could see through the window. She poured a little cold water into the plastic cup resting near the earthenware pitcher and took a sip. As part of her evening ritual she summoned up Umm Ragab, in her imagination, from her bed in the next door block. Then, sitting opposite her, she spoke her mind, in a low voice, about how her neighbour carried on: "Listen, Umm Ragab; your trouble is that you're a donkey. The first day I set eyes on you I said to myself: 'This old woman, with her coarse, red, dyed hair must be a silly ass.' When I first saw you I reckoned you must be well over sixty and you'd have to be an ass to land up in prison at that age. When Mahrousa, the warder, told me what you'd gone down for, I said: 'This old woman must be a fool', because, Umm Ragab, you're in for something so trivial. Three years for stealing a wallet nobody would look twice at with a measly ninety pounds in it – that's thirty pounds for each year of your life in prison. The odd thing is how you owned up, at the investigation, to having been a pickpocket all your life – you said you 'stole to put the flesh on your bones' – and what's more, you're stupid enough to go and tell them how you did it."

As usual, Aziza imagined Umm Ragab sitting in front of her, in the flesh, weeping and trembling as she heard these rebukes; she watched her thin lips, framed by fine folds of skin, which creased up as her small mouth twitched nervously. But Aziza knew that these rebukes were only the outward cause of Umm Ragab's tears; the real cause was the sorrow she felt at not having been able to bid her daughter farewell at her graveside. Moved by such suffering Aziza tried to calm the grieving mother, keeping her image before her in the solitary cell despite the racket coming from next door. Umm Ragab's snoring, which hissed like the escaping vapours of a steam engine, was at that very moment rising to a crescendo and reached Aziza's ears clearly through the open windows. It was hard to believe that this exhausted old woman, sapped of strength by a heart attack that had nearly killed her only hours ago, was sleeping so soundly. It was thanks to Hajja Umm Abdel-Aziz, who gave her heart pills quickly and remained by her side caring for her until the crisis was safely past, that she had survived.

Aziza filled her cup with water; she raised it as if to offer Umm Ragab a drink to stop her crying and calm her down a little. "Enough. Stop weeping, because all these tears, day after day, are taking their toll. Think of yourself for the sake of your poor grandchildren. They're waiting for the day you get out so that you can smother them with your love. You have many hurdles to clear before they're grown up and can fend for themselves and face the world."

Aziza knew very well that nothing would lift the burden of Umm Ragab's sorrow despite her attempts to console her. But she tried to stop her weeping and wailing because she felt her misfortune had no limits. Her only daughter had been widowed a few months before her mother went to prison and then she died, leaving three orphaned children behind, the eldest of whom was only ten. All attempts to save her had failed when the flame of a kerosene stove had caught her long, nylon nightdress which flared up, sticking to her body and turning her into a black, charred lump.

Despite her skinny body and weak heart – which according to the prison doctors threatened to stop at any minute – Umm Ragab never stopped arguing and picking fights with everyone around her. However, since Aziza had learned about her tragedy, she had softened her manner towards her and no longer thought that she was just a wicked old woman. She needed an operation to change two valves in her heart which would, of course, never happen because there was no way Umm Ragab could afford the huge amount needed for a specialist operation of this kind; as for the government hospitals, the queues of those waiting for such operations overflowed into the street.

Aziza put the cup on the floor, tired of holding it up without any response from Umm Ragab. She stubbed out her cigarette butt, and screwed up her eyes a little to examine the woman she still imagined seated in front of her. "I have a surprise for you, Umm Ragab," she said. "A surprise which will make you very happy. But as long as you go on wailing, I'll keep the secret to myself. It's up to you. Wail as much as you like; God willing you'll burst and then you'll only have yourself to blame."

Aziza's face broke into a broad smile revealing her teeth which used to be pearly-white but were now filthy, blackened through neglect and continual smoking. She was revelling in her ability to use her secret as a threat to try and stop Umm Ragab crying and soothe her own tormented soul. So she raised the cup of water and gulped it down as if it were a delicious, mature wine instead of water from the pitcher.

She always took care to fill the pitcher before the cell door was locked behind her in order to make sure she had enough water for the whole night as well as the next morning. She surrendered herself to the delicious stupor which filled her head – a head which still retained traces of a lost beauty – to summon the illusion of drunkenness from that beautiful life she had led in the past, which obsessed her still. She lit herself another cigarette and gazed at the rings of blue smoke rising before her, with the same sad, deep thoughts which often filled her consciousness as she remained alone in her cell, taking her far, far away to her old world, now hidden by bars and walls and long years – long years of solitude in this terrible cell where she sat, longing for the smell of the sea and the distant sound of roaring waves, which she had often heard in her old house. Her spirit yearned to be back in Alexandria, her city, whose architecture had carved vivid reliefs on the walls of her memory.

Aziza the Alexandrian first entered the world of the women's prison before she reached the age of forty, sentenced to life for killing her stepfather, without any reason that the court could ascertain. She insisted on repeating the same statement to explain how she murdered him: as he was sleeping in his bed one night, she slid a sharp kitchen knife into his chest. She claimed that it wasn't he she killed but someone else she found sleeping in his bed. Despite all attempts by the authorities to make her talk and to extract some other statement from her which could mitigate her sentence, she insisted on giving them all the details of how she inserted the knife into the merciless heart of he who had torn her own heart and broken it. She burnt her beautiful memories with him and disposed of all her precious belongings, giving them to a charity for the lepers who begged in the streets of the city and were so obviously in need of care. Then after she killed him and was certain that he had breathed his last breath, she set fire to his photographs and those they shared, to his papers and clothes and to the precious wooden cane with the ivory handle which he used to carry so stylishly. She also set fire to everything else in the beautiful old house with the large, lush garden, which had played host to the lovers, to each moment of their passion and was full of wonderful memories.

Aziza continued to mull over her memories even as she sat in prison – memories which never made her regret what she did because she only killed for the sake of preserving these beautiful, unblemished memories, sweet and pure. The person she killed was not the man she knew so well, who had protected her and raised her from innocent girlhood to the perfectly formed beauty of womanhood. The man she killed was another, with the same features and form as him but without the heart and soul which she had loved with such passion for so long. She was convinced that the man she killed, that other man in his image, who violated her beautiful body before she was even thirteen, was a dangerous criminal who had stolen her loving heart and wasted the passion she poured out for the sake of her love. The man she loved turned out to be a demon in disguise who suddenly revealed himself to her, destroying her happiness and shattering the edifice of tenderness in that old house.

Before the murder she dreamt up many original ways to kill him in a manner befitting the original man she had loved for so long. It was inconceivable that she could kill such a beautiful and noble man in a base, brutish and unseemly way. One time she thought of drugging him heavily so that he couldn't move, then coating him with vast quantities of boiling dark-coloured chocolate until it hardened into an enormous mould of sweetness which no one would be able to resist. She decided to decorate it with dried cherries, sesame and mouth-watering whipped cream. It would then be cut into small pieces with a pick and knife and arranged delicately and tastefully in an amazing spectacle on blue and gold-rimmed sweet trays made from Chinese porcelain. While most of it would be distributed to neighbours and friends, the piece containing that wicked heart, which had once tortured her and left her helpless and despairing of life, would be reserved for herself.

Another time she thought up an alternative way of killing him which might be more suitable. It crystallized in her mind after all those nights spent thinking on her own in the big house, which had become desolate and melancholy – haunted – since her mother died. As she sat on the sofa below her bedroom window gazing at the moon, she could hear only the rustling of the trees and a plaintive sound within her. It was then that she decided to kill him because he was determined to marry that other woman, whom he had begun to love instead of her, and on whom he decided to bestow his new heart. She never believed it was the same heart which had loved her for so many years, from the time she was a little girl, still ignorant of sensations of adult desire. The only method she could think up which fitted her plan to destroy him nobly, was to drug him heavily before he went to sleep and then to bring a huge quantity of rare and beautiful flowers, carefully picked on the morning of the appointed day for the murder. These would be purchased from the best flower shop in the city called "Beautiful Memory" – the very shop from which her lover had bought her violets, narcissi or jasmine during that time of fiery passion which she thought would never end. She would form an arrangement to match his taste in flowers, using white jasmine, birds of paradise with their fan-like veins and magnificent colours in the centre, lavender of mourning and roses from the countryside which she loved, blood red or canary yellow or the colour of his beautiful cheeks which she often used to kiss. She would use her skill in arranging flowers to place them all over him, his head, chest and legs until his body – lying motionless and prostrate after the drug she had administered to him – was completely covered and smothered by their fragrance. Then after she had made completely sure of locking the window and door of the room, letting only the minimum amount of air in, she would leave him to die a slow and beautiful death while he inhaled the lethal fragrance, that familiar scent which she remembered from the beautiful flowers he had given her in the past.

However, Aziza did not use any of the inventive plans she had hatched for a beautiful and truly original murder. She dreaded the scandal that would follow if her secret were found out and her newly created death plan failed, either through lack of precision in its execution or the untimely discovery of her intentions. So she decided to use the knife since it was the quickest and surest way of achieving what she wanted, and gave her the element of surprise which she herself had experienced that day in the distant past when she was still a little girl with pigtails, a little girl whose childhood fate had snatched from her. Like most women she was destined to be a housewife managing the affairs of her narrow world, within the boundaries of four walls, cooking, cleaning and supervising everything to do with the home-bound life which characterizes a woman's existence. On that distant day when her childhood was stolen from her – a day which would never fade from her memory – she was standing in the kitchen preparing dinner for the little family of three made up of herself, her stepfather and her mother, who had just left the house to mourn with some neighbours. While her mother lamented and grieved with the family who had tragically lost their little son, inadvertently swallowed up by the sea, her daughter was pumping the kerosene stove with all her might to try and ignite the flame under the copper pan full of pieces of reddish unripe taroplant, when her stepfather called her. Having returned from work in the afternoon he was sitting on the Istanbuli chair, resting his hand on the arm upholstered with fine English fabric, when he called her to come and take off his shoes, as she usually did. She hurried in from the kitchen and, as she was busy undoing the laces of his soft leather shoes, he suddenly lifted her onto his lap and kissed her over and over again. After a while she realized that his kisses were different from those he used to give her on her cheek – new sensations overwhelmed her little body which should never have experienced such feelings so young – the little body which had not yet ventured beyond the world of innocence.

Since those distant moments, deep in her early childhood, that old man always remained strong, beautiful and fascinating in her mind – even after she slid the kitchen knife into his chest. He was capable of influencing men and women alike and arousing strong emotions, as well as something mysterious akin to fear and awe. Aziza often noticed this effect he had over others from observing all those who had dealings with him, men and especially women, whether at home or when they were out.

On the day of the taroplant incident he told her, while she was still on his lap, that he loved her deeply because she was young and beautiful like one of those mermaids who only appear at night, secretly. Then he asked her to love him just as he loved her and to obey him. He got what he wanted: Aziza continued to obey him as if she were bewitched, her obedience sustained by her infatuation and the compulsive fascination she felt for him. Since those moments in the past, which took place all those years ago but which still remained fresh in her memory even up to the moment she murdered him, she had loved this man passionately, faithfully and wholeheartedly in a way which would be difficult to match. Indeed it was a love so bountiful that it could be divided amongst a thousand women who were devoted in their love. She gave herself, body and soul, because she considered this lover, who had taken her by surprise, no less than an idol, a worshipped god, whose every command must be obeyed, the only person she could ever love. In this way, during those long years, she called him her "worshipped man" which was a secret name only the two of them shared. He was a man who possessed two women, connected to each other through the mother's womb. The three of them lived in that large old house which her mother inherited from Aziza's real father, now dead, and their secret love remained well-guarded and sacrosanct. The mother never knew about it, nor felt the fiery passion between her husband and daughter. She never noticed those impassioned looks and the burning sighs emanating from the depths of the heart and all the drunken kisses in which the lips melted, nor the heated bodily caresses which were deafening in their silence. This ignorance and unawareness was not through lack of sensitivity but because that happy gentle mother, who never for a moment imagined what was going on between her young daughter and her husband in the prime of his manhood, had been blind since birth. Despite this blindness, which fate had ordained for her, her charm and beauty made her attractive to men. She had become extraordinarily lovely, her body beautifully sculptured as if from marble, her eyes flowing with the blueness of the sea, blind to their own beauty. This blindness of hers gave her a certain poetic aura and a touch of humanity and nobility. This aura was brightened when she pinned up her two long, soft plaits forming a beautiful golden crown on her head. Like the queen of an ancient mythic world she reigned with mystery and charm over this old seaside town.

Aziza's mother came from a prosperous family whose men had traditionally worked at the docks. She married a rich man who gave her a child, Aziza, and after his death from typhoid their wealth was combined. She was then free to choose another husband and, because she was still young and had a great deal of money and beauty, her blindness didn't affect her marriage prospects. Many from the city approached her seeking her love and from amongst them she chose the one who became a man to her and to her daughter, Aziza. Aziza was the image of her mother except for a caprice of nature – her skin was slightly brown and her honey-coloured eyes were those of her father –

a living reminder which the mother never saw. Nor did she notice the dreamy, profound look in those eyes with their mysterious seductive quality, bewitching all who looked on her.

Aziza's fateful and early encounter with love and passion hastened her development so that her spirit and the contours of her young body began to resemble that of a mature woman. She joined her mother in bestowing her abundant affection upon the beloved man and her love knew no bounds. Both of them inhabited the narrow world of two women restricted by the four walls of the large, old house and both longed for his return each day. They groomed themselves to the utmost perfection to appear beautiful and exquisite in his sight. In the evening, just like her mother, Aziza would put on pretty nightdresses made out of duchesse satin, crêpe de chine, and shiny satin silk, made by Sonia, the Armenian, the most skilled seamstress in the city. Then she would undo her plaits and let her tantalizing locks of hair tumble onto her shoulders and against her cheeks. As soon as he arrived and was settled in his usual place on the sofa, she would rush to remove his shoes for him. Meanwhile her mother, who would be close by, blessed the interest shown by her beloved husband towards her little daughter. She considered it a measure of good fortune which God, who had often shown her compassion and sympathy, had bestowed upon her in recompense for her blindness. She was thankful for the happiness this new marriage had brought, especially since she had hesitated to remarry for fear of the problems which might arise between her daughter and chosen husband. She had been afraid that she would fall prey to confusion and conflicting emotions, afraid that her peaceful and contented life would turn into a living hell.

However, as time passed in happy days of marriage she was reassured by the wise way in which her husband dealt with her little girl; she valued his care and the intensity of his compassion. Each time he came home he talked affectionately to the child and spoilt her with the expensive presents and treats which gladden the heart of every little girl. She felt extremely grateful for his generosity towards her only daughter and she would tell people that he could never have treated her with the same loving tenderness had she been his own flesh and blood. Nothing disturbed the harmony of the little family over the years and as she sensed the love between her daughter and her husband grow, so her heart was gladdened. She asked God for a long life, and for prosperity for Sheikh Abou El-Mukarim, whom she used to visit in the Perfume Souk and who made her an amulet, which brought happiness to her heart and harmony to the house. She kept the amulet safely in a pouch under her clothes.

What the blind mother never knew was that this family harmony was thanks to charms other than the amulet the Sheikh had written for her with his indelible pencil in a notebook purloined by one of his sons from the Ministry of Education. These were charms which the stepfather used to bewitch his young lover; sumptuous silk lingerie, fit for a film star, ivory hair pins studded with real diamonds, and fine stockings of all sorts of lace and tulle, the like of which the mother had never thought to own. Moreover he bought little games which he played with the young girl to pander to her childish side, a side neglected due to the premature leap she had made into the world of womanhood. Thus Aziza learned, under the instruction of her aged lover, how to hide her abundant charms skilfully without her mother knowing. Those little hidden things were perhaps the only source of Aziza's wrongdoing towards her mother, and made her feel guilty even after her mother died. She regretted keeping these secrets from her since it would have done no harm to have shared the joys and little thrills. When she had suffered enough pain, she began to search for excuses in the fact that she had been very young and in awe of that strong, beautiful man to whom she could only submit.

While this long, protracted relationship with her mother's husband continued, Aziza was able to avoid the dangers which might arise from an illicit love of this kind and instinctively armed herself against all the arrows of love which were directed at her heart from outside. From the time of the taroplant incident these frequently came to take her by surprise. She was blossoming into a mature woman and was the object of desire in a city whose arms had always been outstretched for love, a city in the lap of a sea whose eternal blue doors opened to welcome her into life. From that time on, like a mermaid rising from the sea, she became one of the most eligible girls of the city. She fought off demands from adolescent young men who dreamed of love, as well as those of men capable of paying the marriage price and honouring the commitment of the contract in the normal way and according to the laws of heaven as well as earth. It was rare for Aziza to accompany her mother on visits to relations or friends in the city without there being a prospective fiancé waiting whose mother or sister would urge her mother to discuss the question of marriage. And should they chance to walk along the seashore on a hot, summer's evening she would invariably be followed by footsteps desperate to catch up with her – young men who threw her dreamy, love-crazed glances. But Aziza resisted by bolting the door of her heart. It was as if her lover, her stepfather, had tied her heart to his with a secret invisible thread so that she returned to him despite the temptations of her admirers. It was as if she were under the effects of some dark, magical drug which had made her immune to all the desires which the sultry summer nights aroused and even to the seduction of the crashing waves whose voices, sometimes raging and sometimes gentle, spread the seeds of inflamed love between lovers.

Only once did Aziza nearly fall into the net of love with another man. She went one day to accompany her mother to the gold souk to buy a gold chain with a jewelled pendant. They wandered around the stalls and shops for a while without anything catching her eye until they stopped at a shop which displayed beautiful gold pieces, magnificently worked with jewels and pearls. As Aziza began to examine the displays and described every piece to her blind mother in turn so that she could help her choose something, she caught sight of a young man through the jewellery shop window. He was standing behind the special scales used for the sensitive weighing of gold and was deep in discussion with an old woman sitting opposite about a gold bracelet which had been placed on the scales. Aziza gazed at the young man for a moment, long enough for a bird of crazed love to alight on her soul and steal her heart which began to beat furiously. She followed him, leading her mother into the shop, unable to resist the pull of passion towards this tall man with the captivating face who stood in front of her. He was the kind of man who was irresistible to any woman without any effort on his part. After she had enquired whether she could try on some gold pieces and necklaces she looked at each piece with calculated leisure, describing each one in turn to her mother. She hesitated for so long that her mother, after waiting for more than half an hour without her daughter settling on anything became baffled and finally lost patience. She complained with some irritation that nothing ever pleased her – not even fasting in Ramadan. But the young girl, who hadn't turned sixteen, and who was ignorant of how love begins, was filled with confusion and oblivious to the fact that she was exhausting her mother's patience as a consequence. She finally found something she liked when the jeweller, that "magnet of love" standing in front of her, proposed a truly magnificent gold necklace, made with the conspicuous precision and beauty of skill handed down through generations. In the form of a snake, its little head was studded with tiny, real rubies. He approached her to place it around her long silken neck and fixed the little golden clasp deftly, as an expert merchant should. Aziza's eyes met his, for a long moment, through the large mirror fixed to the wall in front of them. The mirror caught the broken rays of the glistening snake's head resting just at the opening of the bodice of her light blue summer dress. She tilted her head back a little until she brushed his shoulder. When she sensed the rush of blood to his face, tanned from the Alexandrian sun, she felt her heart sink into her shoes.

Her mother sighed heavily at this oppressive silence and announced once more that she was bored of waiting and that her daughter must decide to buy something otherwise they would have to leave the shop. The infatuated young girl announced in a voice, faltering with emotion, that she loved this snake and that the shopkeeper had told her the catch on it needed attention; she would return to collect it in two days time.

Aziza's passionate love for the owner of the golden snake drove her to return to his shop in the jewellery souk two days later. Her heart rate reached a peak when he appeared before her, suddenly, like a bolt of lightning – an incident which would become part of her memory with the same surprising speed. He told her that they were alone in the shop at this early time of the morning because his usual customers – pampered middle class women, reared like hens – were still turning their fat flaccid bodies in their comfortable beds. He then told her of his boundless admiration for her which he had felt ever since he first set eyes on her standing in front of his shop and that his admiration for her had grown after she had come in and talked with him. He then asked about her family and said he was familiar with her background and good reputation. He had decided to marry her because, given that he was a gold merchant whose business had been handed down through the generations from grandfather to father to son, he was worthy of her. His family were extremely prosperous and he would present himself to her, if she wished, that very evening accompanied by his father, his eldest brother and particularly his uncle, without whom no agreement was possible because of his position as head of the family.

Each time Aziza was alone in the large solitary cell, in which the prison authorities had placed her because she was unpredictable and aggressive towards any prisoner who crossed her in the communal wing, she would recall the saga of her extraordinary life, (as if she were watching a long reel of film), and conjure up the people she knew, whom fate had placed in her way. Aziza felt annoyed and ashamed of herself – she was even overcome by her sense of embarrassment – whenever she recalled those moments in which she had stood listening to the one offer of marriage she had considered accepting – something she would regret for the rest of her life.

As she remembered this incident she was filled with shame, and bit her lips again and again until they nearly bled. She felt this because she had allowed herself to be disloyal and had gone beyond the permitted boundaries of her secret world and her unique love. Falling in love with another man to the point of contemplating his offer of marriage – her only one – and the preoccupation with this passion for two days which supplanted her more exceptional love represented the height of self-betrayal and the betrayal of the exquisite world they had shared.

When she returned home after her hasty meeting with the object of this fleeting passion, she thought of her other lover, who at that time was sitting in the government office where he worked as an important official in the council, skilfully handling his papers with the same hands he used to fondle her. She wasn't concerned about her mother's anxiety when she returned empty-handed without the golden snake with the ruby red head, even though her mother was convinced that she had a problem – namely a chronic lack of resolve. Aziza was thinking about one thing only: for two days she had been weaving a mythical love story with the gold merchant, a love touched with pain and suffering because she had resolved to confess the secret of the passion between her and her stepfather. She remained for many hours sitting under her bedroom window, overlooking the garden. She contemplated the white narcissi with their wonderful scent while she imagined the state of the lover, who had fallen head over heels in love, when he learned the details of this illicit relationship. In one image she pictured him having a nervous breakdown, determined to commit suicide and in another he threatened to kill her stepfather – the wolf-man. The climax of her fantasy was the moment he undertook to kill her and to kill himself immediately after so that they might fall, side by side, their blood mingled forever as proof of the union of their souls which would continue after death.

In her cell, Aziza recalled that distant past when she often conjured up numerous pretexts before her mother to deter those who came asking for her hand, in the same way that she used the excuse that she was engaged to a relation of hers when the gold merchant proposed. Aziza would tell her mother that the suitor was ugly and old or that he wasn't suitable socially. On one occasion a young man approached her who was difficult to refuse because he was a model suitor, at least as far as looks are concerned, the likes of whom she would probably never find again. When her mother beseeched her to accept him she used the pretext that a neighbour had told her he preferred the company of men, and his relationships with women were not straightforward. Her mother was later astonished to learn that another young girl, her daughter's friend and neighbour, had married him in a huge wedding ceremony which was the talk of the town for many days after.

Often the lover-husband took part in convincing the mother to reject the men who came forward to her only daughter. Each time she opened the matter he would say, in annoyance, that it was unneccesary and futile to rush her into marriage since she was still a little girl, who had by no means missed the boat. Moreover she possessed the sort of beauty which grew with time, like a precious jewel, and would, with a little patience, enable her to make an excellent match. There was no need to hasten her departure from home since she was the joy of their life and its source of warmth and happiness. Aziza took the same view and complained that her mother wanted her to marry in order to get rid of her and to be done with the matter once and for all. Her mother swore that she only wanted her to get married to secure her future and that if she had the choice, she would have been happy to have Aziza, the joy of her heart, by her side for ever.

For many years after she entered prison, Aziza's amazingly vivid memory preserved the smallest details of her strange life – a memory unrivalled except by that of the Nile eel which remembers the precise details of its journey to the Mediterranean sea where it lays its eggs and breeds. However, as time passed many details fell from the web of her memory. She was no longer completely sure of the kind of knife she used to kill her stepfather nor even of the colour of its handle; was it brown, made of wood from the camphor tree, or black made from fibreglass? Above all she no longer remembered what she drank with her lover on that stormy winter's night during the time of the high *nuwwa* winds when the sky heaped its rain on the city, which withdrew into itself, and the sea crashed against its shores with its huge, mad waves. Was it one of her favourite vintage wines made by Costa, the old Greek, who matured it himself and only sold it to a few of his favoured customers who were connoisseurs? Or was it that strong rum which sent warm currents through the body on cold nights like that night in the distant past? Even though Aziza could not recall such details and kept many others buried in the depths of her memory, she never forgot the conversation they had that night and how, as soon as she had heard his words, she calmly decided to kill him immediately – a decision which led to the murder a few days later.

One day Aziza's mother suddenly contracted meningitis which instead of leaving her with a lasting condition malady like deafness or dumbness – in addition to her blindness – proved to be fatal, leaving her only three more days to live. This was after the doctor had confused her symptoms believing that she had mild influenza from which people often suffered at the end of the summer season and the beginning of autumn. Several years after her mother had departed from this world and as they sat drinking and chatting together, as they did from time to time, Aziza's lover explained to her, after a lengthy preamble, that he couldn't continue to live alone with her under the scrutiny of other people. He wanted to marry again in order to avoid them becoming the subject of rumours. But Aziza knew he was lying and that the threat of gossip was no more than a concealed pretext, like one of the many she had so often used in the past with her mother when she used to pester her about getting married. She knew the truth about his new lover, that he had fallen in love and was no longer able to conceal it despite all his efforts. The compass concealed inside her, able to locate the direction of love, pointed to Nadira, the daughter of his favourite friend, Affat Shahin, one of the best perfume makers in the city. Aziza's jealousy of Nadira knew no bounds and was not surprising since many other women were jealous of her. She was the type of woman who took life as a big game, where everything was open to experience, discovery and risk. She was one of the few women who dared to wear tight helanca leggings when they first came out, exposing her charms in the city streets for all to see; she was also the first girl to dance the hula-hoop in a public place in the city – in the sporting club where she attracted a large circle of young men round her who took pictures of her and whose fascination was fuelled by grateful admiration mixed with scandalized disapproval. Last but not least, she entered into many relationships with boys and men, the youngest of whom was nine years younger than her and the oldest of whom was the husband of Aziza's mother who was twice her age when he fell for her. Nadira spent hours listening to the songs of Abdel Halim Hafez and Faiza Ahmed who were not really well-known at that time but provided a substitute for her unsatiated passion. Their crooning voices sang of the tender love and longing felt by every lover obsessed by his or her latest passion.

• One day Aziza had a dream about Nadira which convinced her that her secret passionate love was about to end. Aziza saw Nadira coming towards her in her dream, dissolving into laughter, while Aziza lay stretched out on her bed, still as a corpse. Then Nadira wrapped her in a shroud with a beautiful piece of rosy silk cloth and placed a garland of thorns on her head. She instructed four tall men in long black cloaks to carry Aziza from her bed and throw her into the sea, at which point Aziza screamed with terror. After this nightmare she stayed in bed until dawn thinking about what it meant and about Nadira. She tried to retrieve the details of how, when her mother died, a relationship developed between them which started the day Affat Shahin arrived with his wife and daughter to pay their respects at the mourning ceremony. Nadira soon became very friendly towards her, surrounding her with tenderness and care as if she were her elder sister, while Aziza became attracted to Nadira because of the ease with which she treated her, avoiding any hint of disharmony – the kind of disharmony women are quick to provoke amongst themselves to cover up their inability to sustain their friendships. This is natural and the result of long years of being unable to exist in their own right in a world where they depend on men. However, Nadira never stopped sniping about Aziza's beauty and her refined manners, during the tedious family evenings when they played cards. These became a regular occasion which Affat Shahin's family would attend with the sad family bereaved of their mother. But in the end, Nadira managed to wreck the close ties and the beautiful friendship which had grown between her and Aziza; she entered the most sacred of all forbidden areas, penetrating the very core of that revered love which lodged in the old secluded house where each corner contained some little detail of their love and under the shelter of which Aziza grew and blossomed. Aziza had known no other love in the world and she had long guarded its secret, carefully and cautiously – a secret which no one, not even her closest relations, ever guessed. On the contrary everyone from the neighbourhood, as well as her relations and friends, perceived their relationship as the model bond based on peace and human serenity which showed that it was possible for a father to feel affection for a child which hadn't sprung from his loins. Aziza grew accustomed to acting two roles with skill as if she had been born to play them. The first role was that of the daughter, grateful to the surrogate father and to her kind and loving blind mother; the second was that of the charming lover immersed to the last atom of her cells in the wide sea of love. Moreover throughout her life, and even after she entered prison and sat in her cell just as she was doing now, she never felt that her two roles were strange or incompatible. Neither did she have any objection to sharing the same man with her mother since she loved her mother very much and felt great fondness for her, helping her to dress and arrange her hair. She chose the most beautiful dresses for her which suited the colour of her skin and her figure, which tended towards plumpness. She continued, to the very end of her mother's life, to choose modern hairdos for her, even advising her to have a page-boy style. She was never reluctant to go with her mother on the occasional visits she paid to the most famous hairdresser in the city, having convinced her that she should dispense with her plaits and that the beautiful new styles brought out the stunning beauty in her face.

By reconciling the two roles in her own mind, Aziza never felt alienated from the person who violated her during that long distant time; in fact as time passed she only grew closer to him. From the time she was a little girl she had regarded him as someone who took care of her. He would bathe her using Nablus soap made from olive oil because it didn't lather too much and so did not hurt her eyes; he would brush her hair and tie it with beautiful ribbons to match the colour of the pretty clothes which he bought from the most splendid children's clothes shops in the city. Before he had sex with her on that unforgettable day she had been used to sleeping in his lap for long periods while he told her stories during which she would take her little worm-shaped fingers and touch his rough, unshaven chin.

Nadira would remain the only woman Aziza would hate and she would hate her for the rest of her life because, in her opinion, Nadira was a thief, an adulteress, a liar and a murderer who had destroyed her joy. In fact she was the storm whose evil force invaded the seven pillars of happiness which had supported her. She had snatched her husband from her, her lover and darling, her brother, father and friend and she had uprooted her from the past, present and the future without conscience or mercy.

Nadira was less beautiful than Aziza in all respects and she was not as well proportioned. Her body, for example, was impaired by her broad shoulders and a rather high waist but she had a strong personality, as well as being kind and capable. She made the best of her good points and was able to conceal her weak ones to the extent that she appeared, to all who saw her, to be a radiant, seductive woman who aroused men's desire to possess her and wrest her away from other men. But above all else, the considerable degree of learning Nadira had obtained enhanced her distinction and presence. She had been to university for a time but, since she did not particularly enjoy studying, she left with the hope that she could take up painting. This was in contrast to Aziza who had barely completed her primary education, and whose worldly knowledge had never been sharpened because her experience had been limited to a life of perpetual isolation in the large house with her blind mother, deprived of any brothers and sisters with whom she could have shared the details of daily life.

Aziza had often noticed the impression Nadira made when she came in or when she was present in some place or other. She felt jealous and frustrated when people paid attention to her and spoke to her while excluding Aziza or when men, sitting in their corners, changed places to get near her. Nadira was blessed with intelligence and was very articulate. She wasn't put out by Aziza's anger and continued to praise her in a way which was quite genuine. She even steered the conversation so that Aziza could take some part in it. But one day when Nadira and her stepfather stayed up all night in the house playing cards she sensed that he was playing a role other than that of hospitable host. It was then that she knew that her lover had fallen for that dark, attractive girl.

The widower and lover took personal charge of preparing food for Nadira and closely studied all the movements which she used to show off her feminine charms. He listened extremely attentively, hanging on her every word, and the words they exchanged were accompanied by impassioned looks.

After that Aziza thought that Nadira would be like a summer cloud passing fleetingly across the sky of her peaceful relationship with her stepfather, like all those clouds which had passed by during their long relationship. There were the dancers in the city nightclubs and the pretty Italian lady whose picture he left scattered amongst the papers on his desk at home. This lady gave him many presents and souvenirs and Aziza never knew that he in turn gave her a little boy whom she took with her abroad after the cosmetics factory where she worked was nationalized. But Aziza's hopes were dashed the moment he told her of his intention to marry Nadira, despite the fact that he was around sixty years old, for she had never thought that he would contemplate marriage again. Perhaps it was because his handsome face, unmarked by wrinkles, belied his true age that he was encouraged to take a step of this kind – added to which he considered Nadira a real catch. So when he set out to convince Aziza that this arrangement would be preferable for them both and began to discuss the practical details of his intended marriage, especially those concerning the house and its rooms, Aziza was convinced that his intention to marry was serious. She stared at him, without blinking an eye, while she thought about the most suitable way to kill him.

Aziza's symptoms of madness gradually appeared a few years after entering prison. At first they revealed themselves through her habit of talking to herself from time to time in a way which was incomprehensible to the other prisoners because she spoke in the few Greek words she learned from Umm Zakhary, her Cypriot neighbour. Aziza always took great pains to avoid placing herself in a position in which her dignity would be exposed to their abuse. But after her symptoms emerged, it became noticeable that she lost much of the arrogance and haughtiness which she normally displayed towards those she came across in prison, even towards the warders themselves who treated her with caution. She distributed her clothes to anyone who needed them, keeping only the bare minimum for herself. Finally she started hitting any prisoner who annoyed her or contradicted her and once she almost hit Mahrousa, the warder, who would have given her a slap hard enough to lay her out on her bed like a corpse. However Mahrousa had a kind heart and she remembered that Aziza had given her a magnificent black lace nightdress only two days before so she thought better of it and cajoled her into returning to her cell. But one day Aziza attacked and bit Lula, the procuress, very hard because when they met in the prison corridor Lula told her that she should have met her outside the prison ten years ago and she would have sorted her out. Finally, after all possible methods of punishment in the prison had failed to restrain her the prison authorities decided to bring her before the prison psychiatrists. She appeared before two young doctors who came to assess her case. In their report they described her as calm and gentle – as someone who conversed with the confidence of one of the princesses of the deposed Alawite family and whose civilized manners and aristocratic appearance were proof of her high social standing. This earned her their respect and they decided, in the end, and after long discussions with her, that she was not mad at all. Nevertheless their decision was perhaps more a measure of the madness they frequently encountered in their professional lives far outside the prison walls.

The prison authorities were content to confine Aziza to a solitary cell inside the prison hospital, next to the ward for the weak and disabled, and perhaps that was the most compassionate decision taken on her behalf since she had been sentenced for life after killing her stepfather. In contrast to her previous life in the communal ward, the new arrangement suited her well, because at last she was able to spend long, peaceful evenings on her own, without any disturbance or harassment from anyone sharing her space. She could stay up at night alone, gazing at the stars for long periods of time, without anyone asking her to close the wooden window so that the stray cats and the insects didn't creep in. Here she would spend her nights thinking with serenity and precision about all those whom she would take with her on the beautiful golden chariot with magnificent white, winged horses ascending to heaven, and which she insisted should include only the most distinguished and noble women of the prison. For these women were really angels without wings who had lost their way to heaven and come instead to this awful, depressing solitary place from which she would rise with them, returning them to their rightful place above by means of that magnificent chariot. The magnificence of the chariot was greater even than that of King Farouk, which she had seen one morning moving through the streets of the city when he arrived from his seaside palace in Muntaza. She was sitting now, after thinking a great deal about the matter of Umm Ragab, having decided to include her in the celestial voyage up to heaven.

Aziza had never liked Umm Ragab who, in her opinion, was the very embodiment of vulgarity and crookedness. Since the day Umm Ragab first came to the prison, sentenced to three years after being accused of picking pockets, Aziza had avoided having any dealings with her because she hated her demonic appearance. Umm Ragab had a small aged face, full of fine wrinkles, and red hair which was almost light orange from too much dyeing with henna. This thick, frizzy tousled mop of hair made her look as if the eternal flame had settled on her head. However, the way Aziza saw this head was different, and somewhat strange. She felt it resembled a little, rotten melon with decayed skin which had darkened. Perhaps this was due to the vile, putrid smell which clung to Umm Ragab, about which Aziza made rude comments every time she passed or approached her. In addition to this, Aziza felt unnerved by her harsh, quick, nervous glances; her eyes darted about like those of a little fox. Aziza's observation was accurate because these were looks which distinguished pick-pockets from other thieves. Her extremely thin fingers and her skinny hands were another indication that she was a professional who picked wallets, money and precious things from their rightful place in people's pockets or handbags.

Umm Ragab was not descended from a family of professional pickpockets and she had never had formal tuition but she was, nevertheless, extremely skilled. She took it up as a profession with ease sometime after her husband had divorced her barely five months after their marriage; soon after that, she gave birth to his daughter and was forced to fend for herself to meet her daily needs and those of her little child.

• The nub of Umm Ragab's story – and this was the name by which she liked to be called by all the prisoners – was the dream she nurtured of mothering another child – a male – whom she would call Ragab. This was one of the small wishes she had cherished in her former life outside prison and which she had tried unsuccessfully to realize by attaching herself to any man who would agree to marry her, whatever his circumstances and no matter how poor. She once even lured an old beggar, whom she saw roaming the streets, crawling along the ground because he had lost both legs. She offered to shelter him in the little room where she lived with her daughter and the man agreed because he had no fixed dwelling. He used to spend his nights in some mosque or other or with some of his prosperous beggar friends who owned houses and provided shelter for a fee. After the man moved into her house, Umm Ragab was happy and felt that she was quite close, or closer, to realizing her wish – of having Ragab. She almost broached the question of marriage when she felt sure of the old man and had showered him with as much of her ill-gotten gains as she could. She did very well in her trade due to favourable circumstances made possible through the inefficiency of government planning, which meant that the city had become inundated with people who, day after day, poured into the city from the villages and little towns which lacked most of the basic services. This gave Umm Ragab the opportunity to increase her takings under cover of the crowds of people crammed into the public buses, and especially the trains, which operated between the centre of town and the distant suburbs. But Umm Ragab was confused when she discovered a little boy sleeping contentedly next to the old beggar, when she returned late one night after a very active day due to the celebrations at the end of Ramadan. At this time of the year, most people working in the government and the public sector went out to buy clothes and new shoes for members of their families after they had been paid their bonus. Umm Ragab was convinced that the hope she had pinned on this man to grant her the dear little gift, Ragab, had been dashed. At that moment, and without any discussion, she threw him out of the house, ahead of his little boy, after stripping him bare of his most treasured possessions; a cross-over lady's jacket and a white skull cap made of lamb's wool. She had bought them both especially for him from a shopkeeper who sold second-hand clothes, without realizing, of course, that the jacket was meant for a woman because it was one of those you saw around in the seventies when it was fashionable for women to wear men's clothes. She categorically refused his entreaties to remain for the night and to let him pay back half the amount of the jacket, just as she stood firm in the face of her daughter's pleas to let the boy stay the night with them so that they could play a little together.

Perhaps Umm Ragab's failure in realizing her simple, modest desire – which is one that many women achieve every day – was the cause of her complex and her perpetual sense of frustration. It might also have accounted for her unique ability to transform the simplest of problems into huge tragedies. For instance, if she let the milk boil over on the stove or if her daughter let a cup fall on the floor she screamed and howled as if some terrible calamity had befallen her. Then with the passing of time she changed into a malicious person with negative feelings towards everyone, making her an ideal spy for the prison warders. She went to extreme lengths to flatter them and to ingratiate herself with them through informing them about every detail which took place in the cells, whether she witnessed it herself or heard about it some other way. She didn't hesitate to report any prisoner who tried to contravene the internal regulations of the prison. For example, one of the prisoners might hide a mirror or some simple cosmetics, or it might be a coloured dress which she would conceal and put on at night when there was only one warder on duty, or two at the most, usually sleeping deeply at this time. However, none of this changed the fact that, for as long as the opportunity presented itself, Umm Ragab continued to carry out the activities which had landed her in prison and which had always laid her open to problems when she was outside. Aziza bumped into her for the first time when she noticed her trying to steal a boiled egg which she had just placed next to some olives resting on a piece of bread on a window ledge, ready for breakfast. As she stood outside the room stretching her hand towards it, Aziza, who was standing inside washing a tomato to have with her food, grabbed hold of her and descended on her with a fierce bite which would have torn a bit of flesh from Umm Ragab's hand if it hadn't been for her scream which immediately brought several prisoners to rescue her hand from Aziza's teeth, while Aziza continued to curse and swear with rage. Then instead of eating the egg and olives with the bread, Aziza threw it all into the prison courtyard because she declined to eat food which Umm Ragab had coveted to the point of stealing. But Aziza had a deeper reason than that for hating Umm Ragab since she had discovered that she had a pathological aversion to soap and water, no doubt accounting for the vile, putrid smell which wafted over everyone who came near her. Even though the warders forced Umm Ragab to take a bath from time to time the parasitic fungi, which thrived in the summer, became more vigorous after each time she bathed and multiplied between her toes, her fingers and under her arms and between the folds of her skin encouraging this unbearable smell to flourish.

• But on this memorable day, such as the prison had never witnessed before, Aziza's opinion of Umm Ragab underwent a change so radical as to be on a par with Gallileo's revolutionary theory of the rotation of the earth around the sun. Aziza was roused from her usual afternoon nap by the shrieks and wails of Umm Ragab, who had just been informed by the prison authorities of her daughter's death after a huge fire had broken out in her home. She occupied a single room in a block in which the owner rented out communal rooms to the poor – people in the city who were unable to rent privately and who were forced to share one room with their family. Umm Ragab continued to cry and mourn for her daughter who died in the fire, leaving her three children behind. A man who lived next door and made his living selling popcorn from a cart had been trying to fill his gas cylider when it exploded, spreading gas through every corner of the house which then burst into flames.

The daughter who died in the fire had been standing in her room frying aubergine and potatoes for her three daughters who were playing hopscotch in the street at midday. Umm Ragab's despair increased whenever she remembered the fate of these little girls; only months ago they had lost their father, a chronic diabetic, when he was struck down by a fatal attack after eating two large pieces of *konafa* cake.

The thought of this tragedy drove Umm Ragab to strike her face in lamentation and to scream for hours with an amazing amount of energy. Her cheeks, puffed out and swelled up engulfing her narrow, fox-like eyes. Finally, when she was capable of expending no more feelings of grief or misfortune she fell in a swoon.

Aziza remained on her bed in her cell and suffered for Umm Ragab in her grief which she felt in all its strength through hearing all the wailing and face-slapping that penetrated through the open window of her cell from the ward next door. For the first time, Aziza's eyes were opened to the truth of Umm Ragab's existence, the most wretched of people she knew, a woman who had been devoured by suffering and now wasn't even able to see her daughter to say her final farewell at the grave. The weight of her enormous pain would continue to burden her and consume her spirit whenever she thought about the three young ones who were cut off without a mother or father to care for them, while she was far away, unable to do anything for them and unable to drive away the evil which had befallen them.

Aziza wept real tears out of the intense sympathy she felt for Umm Ragab, and in these moments she tried to justify her existence as a thief and pickpocket because Umm Ragab had gained nothing through her life of picking pockets nor did she derive glory from it; nothing she accumulated during the days of poverty and hardship was of direct benefit to her. Instead she stole and picked pockets to live and eat and perhaps if she had found a better means of earning a living she would not have stolen.

After that Aziza felt that she had gone too far in her sympathy for Umm Ragab because thieves are thieves, whatever, and they must be punished for it. However while turning the matter over in her mind, she remembered her stepfather, and remembered Nadira and was convinced that, despite everything, there was no justice in this world and if she had the scales of justice in her hand then she would place Nadira in the place of Umm Ragab, and put her stepfather in her place. There are crimes of conscience which human laws fail to rectify. Here was Umm Ragab serving a sentence in prison but in reality it was like being sentenced to death because she couldn't even take a last look at her daughter who was lying dead, would never be able to hug her or cry on her shoulder or even plant a final goodbye kiss on her cheek.

Aziza continued to cry for Umm Ragab and felt how harsh she had been on her. She reproached herself strongly inside because she had not let her steal the egg and the olives with bread but instead bit her until she made a toothmark on her wrist which looked like a round, blue watch, remaining on her flesh for many days after. Then Aziza lit herself a cigarette and got up to walk around her cell. She continued to reproach herself strongly and realized how thoughtless it would be not to take Umm Ragab with her in the golden chariot up to heaven. Because, before this incident, the very thought of Umm Ragab's dirty hand contaminating that magnificent heavenly chariot which Aziza had drawn in her imagination, had been inconceivable. The chariot was an exact replica of the royal golden coach which she had once seen long ago, with a simple modification; a collection of strong, outstretched wings which would raise its six beautiful white horses on the ascent up to heaven and through the gap in the billowing clouds.

• This incident was not the only reason which made Aziza change her mind about excluding Umm Ragab from the golden chariot. There were other aspects which made Aziza decide on the matter irrevocably. Even though Umm Ragab was a professional pickpocket, as she later admitted to Aziza, she had never stolen unless she was desperate. After her husband left her she had tried to find any work which would earn enough to stave off her hunger and that of her daughter. One time she worked in a leather tannery where she had to clean the buffalo and calf skins of hair and for her hard labour, which went on throughout the day, she was paid a paltry sum – hardly enough for them to live on. In addition, the disease which she contracted, mycosis, would not have been difficult to cure if only Umm Ragab could have afforded to buy the ointment which would cure this cursed fungus. Another time she bought packets of candy floss from a wholesaler and sold it to children for a small profit. But the problem was that she was compelled to eat what was left over at the end of the day since her feet were tired from doing the rounds and her empty stomach was racked with hunger. Then she sold balloons and roasted corn and worked for a long time as a porter in the vegetable souk, lugging heavy sacks of potatoes and tomatoes until one day she suffered a slipped disc which prevented her from working. If it hadn't been for a few potatoes which she occasionally stole from the big sacks, she and her daughter would have perished from hunger like animals and it was for this reason that she finally took to picking pockets as a profession, even though it happened quite by chance. One day she was standing in front of the crowded co-op trying to buy a packet of rice when she caught sight of the open handbag belonging to a woman standing in front of her in the queue, probably one of the government employees who do their shopping at the end of their working day. The bag had a little leather purse in it and Umm Ragab stretched out her thin hands, calmly snatched it and slipped it down the front of her dress as she slid away from the queue. It was true that she only found three pounds in it but the joy it gave her knew no bounds since on the very same day she bought a tin of sesame halva, half of which she ate with her child, a kilo of tangerines, and a kilo of macaroni all of which gave her the strength to face another day or two. For Umm Ragab the three pounds provided an unforeseen opening to the world of picking pockets. She remained an independent agent during her professional life, refusing to join any of the associations which specialized in the trade and which are widespread in some parts of the city. After they started talking to each other, Umm Ragab confessed to Aziza that she weakened on one occasion and almost joined a gang which pursued their activities on a large scale in buses transporting passengers between Cairo and other districts. But she changed her mind after she thought hard and realized that picking pockets on her own was infinitely preferable because if one of the gang fell into the hands of the police, it was probable that he would give the rest of them away. However, this decision to go it alone frequently cost Umm Ragab dearly because she was forced to be on the alert at all times, not only to the gangs which often stole from the areas in which she operated, but also to the scrutiny of the police. Then she told Aziza how one time she was nearly killed by some members of a gang who, when they discovered that she was practising her trade on territory mapped out for them according to an agreement with the other gangs, resented her persistent refusal to join them. This gang then kidnapped her and took her to a deserted spot far from the city. Some of them began throttling her but she begged them so piteously to let her return to her only daughter who was completely dependent on her that they contented themselves with giving her a violent beating. This left a scar above her left eyebrow but it was hardly visible because of the many wrinkles on her face.

Aziza had learned all the details of the tragic end which landed Umm Ragab in prison after a period of reconciliation between them, and this was the factor which finally outweighed all others in deciding to include her in the group of people to go in the heavenly golden chariot. Aziza, who knew about fate from experience and understood the games it plays, realized, after much thought and close examination of Umm Ragab's case, that it had played these games only to ensure that she would be included with those who were going to heaven. Because despite the precision with which Umm Ragab carried out her work and her extreme caution and amazing talent as a pickpocket, nevertheless, the government caught her in a way that could only be described as fateful. One day she was working on the underground in Masr Jadida, which she considered one of the most lucrative sites for withdrawing money from the pockets of the long-suffering passengers who were slow to start in the morning. She succeeded in removing a colourful pearl-studded purse – the kind made in Taiwan, which women are mad about and which became widespread after Egyptians went to the Gulf where these sort of goods are ten a penny, like the artificial silk blouse appliqued with pearls which the young owner of the purse was wearing. But she wasn't paying attention to her handbag and, while the young woman was busy arranging the loose strands of her hair with her painted fingernails, Umm Ragab opened it with the utmost facility and skill gained from practising her trade for more than thirty years. The operation was successful. Umm Ragab turned round after quickly hiding the purse in a plastic bag containing some vegetables and bread, but while she was preparing to get off safely at the next stop, a suckling baby, in all innocence, got hold of the bread with its tiny fingers, exposing the purse which was underneath it. It was Umm Ragab's bad luck that the owner caught sight of it immediately since she had just turned round to stand behind Umm Ragab in order to get off at the same stop.

A pile of cigarette ends had gathered in front of Aziza. One of her headaches, which afflicted her from time to time because she suffered from high blood pressure, started again. She had thought enough and had turned the question of Umm Ragab over thoroughly in her mind. She got up to walk a little and to prepare something to eat because she had begun to feel hungry. Looking up at the high ceiling of her room where spiders had installed themselves in every corner she raised her hand to say good evening to one of them, adding that it was better off than her because it had come to this place of its own free will. Then she asked it to do a simple, but extremely important, favour for her which was to go quietly to Umm Ragab and whisper in her ear saying: "Aziza told me to tell you . . . Alright . . . She's going to take you up there if she's around to do it, God willing."

2

The Heart of the Matter: the Meeting of Opposites

The real, hidden reasons behind old Hinna's killing of her husband, who was about four years older than her, remained a secret which she kept from everyone including her three children and the judges. Hinna stuck to her first statement before the prosecution – adding nothing to it. She claimed that she had forgotten about the container of water she had placed on the gas stove which had boiled dry after she and her husband had gone to sleep that evening. She added that when she woke up the next morning she found herself in a drugged state, unable to move or even breathe normally, and when she called her husband to help her get out of bed he didn't answer, even though she called him repeatedly. She became aware of a strong smell of gas all over the house and it was then that she remembered the container which she had placed on the burner before she went to sleep. She pulled herself together and rushed to the kitchen to discover gas escaping from the burner which had gone out all that time ago. However the judges and prosecution received Hinna's testimony with complete scorn and derision; the many gaps in her statement and the numerous clues and corroboration arising from the investigation, to which the prosecution had access, in their view merely established premeditation. As a result she went down for ten years for premeditated murder despite the strenuous efforts made by the lawyer hired by her children to defend her. He had urged her to say that her husband beat and tormented her and was stingy towards her, driving her to her wit's end, and that she had been treated unjustly by everyone. He wanted her to tell them that she killed him in a moment of rage and that she now bitterly regretted the terrible deed she had committed against the person closest to her, and to beg the judges to look on her case with sympathy and mercy because she had confessed to her crime and was full of remorse and grief which was crushing her spirit. However Hinna stuck to her first statement and closed her ears to the lawyer's advice considering his interference in this matter as a sort of dim-wittedness, also ignoring the entreaties of her children who, she felt, had spent money recklessly on the lawyer's fee. She pursed her thin lips resolutely, drawing them into a hollow into which the fine wrinkles in the area surrounding them disappeared. This transformation made the judge, who yawned with boredom throughout the long drawn-out speeches on behalf of the defence and the prosecution, decide on a sentence which seemed quite lenient, given that he didn't condemn her to life imprisonment or to death as is common in such cases. He justified this on the basis that she was old and suffered from a heart condition and high blood pressure, as confirmed by the medical report which her lawyer had submitted as evidence on her behalf. Since there was every indication that her death was not far off he decided to leave the matter to Azrael, the angel of death. In fact fate was to determine the opposite since Hinna lived to serve out half her time and came out into the world once again after the Government declared an amnesty on the occasion of the celebration of the Revolution in which she and other prisoners were included. The feeling of optimism she felt at the moment she heard her sentence may have been behind the faint smile playing on her lips which occasioned the irritation of prosecuting counsel; he had described her, at an earlier stage, in the most unpleasant and debased terms.

It happened that Hinna's place in the women's prison, in the communal ward for the old and weak, was next door to the single cell allocated to Aziza the Alexandrian. Hinna won Aziza's love and approval soon after she met her. The day after Hinna was brought to prison she was in the bathroom by the hand basin, jumping up and trying to reach the tap to turn it on. But because it was high up and she was so short she found it an impossible task. Aziza offered to help her by turning on the tap and, thanking her, Hinna laughingly referred to her shortness which had so often brought her trouble in her dealings with people and continually made her the subject of jokes. Her husband had even refused to walk by her side when they went out together – he was rather tall – and forced her to walk a few steps behind him until they reached their destination.

Aziza really liked Hinna and invited her to eat breakfast with her in her solitary cell. The two women sat down to eat what was available – the macaroni left over from the day before which Jamalat, the thief, had cooked for Aziza after she had stolen a small tin of sauce from the prison kitchen. As they shovelled bits of macaroni into their mouths with spoons and nibbled a green onion which she had washed, Jamalat stood in a corner of the room waiting for the water to boil. She had poured this into a small clay jug on the cheap electric cooking element with spiral wires so that she could make some of the strong sweet Kushary tea which Aziza preferred and which was the only thing that helped her morning headaches. While they were eating with relish Hinna related to Aziza simply and fluently, as if she were telling the story of a good film she had recently seen, the really peculiar story of life with her husband which led her, in the end, to the women's prison. She told it without a hint of anger or apparent regret; as she recounted the details of the story she appeared to be extremely happy since she would smile from time to time, showing her teeth which were beautifully white for no other reason than they were false. Her youngest son had paid to have them made by one of the most famous specialists in the whole Republic. Hinna was able to draw Aziza to her exciting story and Jamalat also listened to her with ardent zeal because in the first place the tale was well worth listening to and secondly because she wanted to memorize the details and tell it to her friends in the scabies ward to pass the time and relieve the boredom. Jamalat was so intent on Hinna's words and distracted by them that she didn't notice the water was boiling furiously until it spilled over onto the little heating element. The thin coil had become red hot and made a loud sizzling noise as the water touched it and evaporated immediately.

As Hinna narrated her story to Aziza, the first person to hear it since she killed her husband, she discovered a truth which she hadn't thought of during all the long years of her life: that she had to free herself from the husband with whom she had lived for about forty-five years before she had dared to kill him. Perhaps it was a stroke of good luck that she recognized this truth after she had grown old because if she had killed him when she was much younger than she was now, the court, which had been concerned by her age and state of health, might not have entrusted her fate to Azrael and would have handed down the usual punishment for such a crime – the death penalty, or at the very least a life sentence.

Hinna was prepared to tell her story, not only to Aziza, but to any other prisoner who asked her. Even if she wasn't close to them or naturally at ease with them she tried to get to know them, as she did with Aziza. However, she was never prepared to discuss this matter with any man, however close he was to her, even with one of her sons. The same had applied to her own lawyer or the judge himself, even if he should have decided to pass sentence to have her cut into tiny pieces and thrown to the dogs in the street, because it was impossible for someone like her, blessed with a correct and refined upbringing, to talk about personal matters concerning what goes on between men and women in the bedroom. Even among women, before she carried out the murder, she had not been prepared to speak about a matter of this nature, however much anger and exasperation she had suffered as a result and however great the desire to unburden the feelings which rose within her. When all was said and done, everyone must accept his lot in life: her husband had met his end as ordained by God, and she had taken up residence in the strange world of the women's prison. As matters stood, she no longer cared and nothing prevented her from narrating her story, from start to finish, to anyone who asked, because she felt no shame or embarrassment in the presence of another woman who had the same body as her, shared similar feelings to her, and was able to understand, feel and evaluate all she had suffered in her life and had been unable to express when she lived with her late husband.

• Hinna told Aziza about her husband's insatiable appetite for the opposite sex, which she had discovered that day, long ago when she was married off to him. The insane urge which impelled him to have sex with her on their wedding night no less than nine times, despite the terrible pain that she suffered and which made her beg him to desist from the painful act that made her feel as though she was going to die. But instead of responding to her tormented pleas, he persisted in violating her over and over again until daybreak, by which time she was in such agony that she spent a whole hour sitting in a tub filled with warm water, with half a spoonful of salt added to it, until the pain had subsided a little. While she sat in the tub, a desperate desire to sleep overcame her; her head dropped onto her chest and she fell into a deep slumber.

At noon the next day, when her mother and father came, accompanied by her younger sister, to congratulate her on the first morning of her life in her happy marital home, she wished she could spit on them all and hit her mother whom she considered, at that moment, primarily responsible for the greatest crime ever – for it was her mother who had been behind her marriage to that stallion, that amazingly potent man who required, not only one woman, but a huge number of females, to jump on them all the time like a cock amidst the hens in the pen. She might have lashed out, spitting and hitting, under the influence of the glass of wine suddenly forced on her by her husband as an antidote to the wounds he had inflicted upon her and which still traumatised her. However, instead of behaving in any of these rather discourteous ways towards her family, who were as close to her as anyone could be – especially her mother who had carried her in her womb for nine months – she composed herself and forced back her anger. Without forgiving them, she painted a false smile of joy on her lips as befits a bride on the first day after her marriage. She was convinced that the axe had fallen on her head and that in everyone's eyes, including the eyes of the State and those of her parents, she had become the wife of this man whose face overflowed with happiness as he welcomed her family warmly, the husband of their daughter who was receiving them in his marital home for the first time.

Hinna braced herself and prepared the table for the lunch which her mother had cooked and brought with her in an endeavour to please her and to avoid inconveniencing the new husband. But while they were all listening to one of the excellent radio shows which were being broadcast at the time, the husband stood up and went into the bedroom. He then called Hinna to come and when she joined him he locked the door behind them and caught her unawares with a quick bout, taking advantage of the fact that the guests still had their ears glued to the radio. However, the guests soon became aware of the absence of the married couple and, feeling their presence had become an imposition, called out their best wishes to the happy couple, placing some money as a token for the lovebirds in a small envelope on top of the radio – which they forgot to turn off – and left for home.

Since that far off time, and throughout the long years, Hinna had been her husband's mare, at his disposal day and night. Sometimes he surprised her by returning from work earlier than usual and she would then have to drop anything she was doing in the house to go to bed. For that reason the food, which she was preparing for lunch, often burnt in the little pot on the stove and in spite of herself, much to her embarrassment she would drop the washing which she was folding or hanging out on the line to join him in bed. Despite the fact that she soon bore him three children, who were enough to gladden any melancholy heart, he was not deflected from his sexual desire for Hinna's weakened body; she even had to leave her screaming suckling child while she attended to his father's sexual needs. The whole business became a problem which took up hours of Hinna's day; she adopted the boy scouts motto: "Be prepared!" to be ever alert for these marital demands. She would bathe, put kohl on her eyes, powder on her cheeks. She would expose as much as possible of her arms and breasts over which he liked her to let her beautiful black hair hang loosely, like a frisky young filly. In this way she would appear, as he always wanted her, like a tart in one of those nightclubs which had spread all over the city and not like a wife from a good family or an exemplary mother who never took her eyes off her children except when compelled to attend to the needs of her troublesome husband.

All that Hinna was forced to endure made her feel disdain for the instructions and advice her mother had given her before her marriage, and continued to give, concerning domestic matters, insisting that she should keep the house in perfect order. It was advice which she often wished she had the time to follow. Instead, the apartment had become more like a doss house than a comfortable family home.

She always tried to avoid looking exhausted or grubby when she did the housework. Anyone visiting the house noticed the strange discrepancy between the care she took over her grooming and personal cleanliness and the dirt which accumulated on the Belgian mirror with its beautiful, golden frame where the details of the fine engraving were masked by the layer of dust which had settled on it. Dust covered everything in the room, even the five peacock feathers in the Chinese vase which stood on the marble-topped table with golden inlay and golden cabriole legs. The kitchen had spiders on the ceiling and cockroaches lived in the cracks of the wooden cupboards, confident that they would not be disturbed by the invasion of some super rotating cleaner or deadly insecticides. Such facts testified to the lack of interest the mistress of the house showed in her home and the lack of priority she gave it, since her prime function in life was to make herself available to her husband and to provide the conditions in which he might pursue his habitual activities at any time he desired.

Hinna tried to the best of her ability to curb the exuberance of her husband's libido through different devices. When her children were small she used to take them for extended visits to her mother's house which lasted from morning till evening in the hope of snatching some time far away from her untameable stallion. But when he discovered that she was away from home for a whole morning it was more than he could bear and he followed her to her mother's to fetch her home quickly. On one occasion he was too impatient to wait until they got home and took her to the bathroom in her mother's house, locking the door behind them without the slightest feeling of shame despite the fact that his children were screaming outside, alarmed at the strange behaviour of their parents. Had her mother not been out of the house at the time Hinna would have felt deeply embarrassed. Another tactic, Hinna adopted was playing cards and backgammon in the evenings which he was so determined to spend with her at home, but this also failed miserably since all he desired was to pass the time playing his own favourite game. When the children grew up their financial needs increased to an extent which could no longer be met from his small salary, so Hinna bought a knitting machine and took refuge in her nightly occupation while he would be begging her to come to bed. However, he became exasperated by the attention she paid to the machine rather than him. Unfortunately the machine was not a sturdy 'Singer' but a shoddy Japanese make, one of many that had flooded the market, and when he hurled it to the floor in a rage, it broke.

Just as her plans for card games, backgammon and the knitting machine all failed, only to be replaced by the delights of tawdry sex magazines which gave her husband ideas for new positions to try with his beautiful but ageing wife, so Hinna's attempts to restrict the number of times he had sex with her also failed. Once she put sleeping pills in the glass of warm milk and honey which he loved to drink in the evening, but although he lay like a corpse until the next morning, he had hardly awakened to the world around him and had not even opened his mouth, before his hand stretched out to touch her body and he descended on her, doubly refreshed after hours of deep sleep.

Only once did Hinna feel that her problems with this husband of hers might be resolved, when his work took him away to a coastal town several hours from Cairo by train. But after only a week, during which she was able to sleep calmly without sudden attacks, her husband paid a bribe to be posted back home. The bribe was half her savings, collected over two years to buy a television like the rest of the neighbours because she was the only one in the block who didn't have one.

After that Hinna became convinced that there was nothing to be done and considered her husband's nature to be a lost cause or rather her ordained fate, which had been inscribed on a tablet in heaven, even before the seed had been deposited in her mother's womb. Indeed her mother had told her one day that God keeps a tablet for everyone on which is written all that is and all that will be for that person from birth until death. She even hoped for some miracle to happen which would make her husband fall ill and curb his over-developed zeal for his marital duties, or that he would suffer some permanent physical disability which would keep him away from her. However, at times she would console herself that her troubles might have been much worse had her husband been one of those men who attach themselves to other women. He was a petty official with a limited income; if she had not been able to budget and economize, then the family could not have survived. It was probable that had he sought the acquaintance of some other woman, he would have appropriated a portion of his salary to provide for this woman, to buy her gifts and take her around and about, all of which would have threatened the stability of her family life.

Eventually, Hinna gave up all hope and convinced herself that such problems would only be solved with time. But she reached the age of fifty only to be proved wrong. For although she was on the threshold of old age and her three children had married and left to set up their own homes, and although her own sexual desires had lessened, this was not the case as far as her husband was concerned. For him they increased, now that he was unburdened from the worries of children and was free to devote himself to his relationship with her. Moreover, he insisted that she use face powder and scent and that she wear skimpy nightdresses more suited to a girl on her wedding night. These he could afford thanks to the periodic rises in his pay and because the children had grown up and were beginning to be responsible for themselves. What particularly angered and exasperated Hinna were his persistent demands to let her hair hang loosely onto her shoulders, leaving a little fringe on her forehead to enhance her captivating cheeks, even though her hair had become thin as a result of pregnancies, breast-feeding and the passing of time as well as through all the dyeing and using of curlers ever since she was a young girl, engaged to be married. She tried to convince her husband that there was no need for the fringe and that it would be much better for her to have it cut it at the hairdressers in a way which was better suited to someone of her age, with hair in the condition it was, but he refused categorically, telling her he would buy her some oil to strengthen the roots of her hair from one of the largest and best-known perfume makers renowned for his skills. Moreover he refused absolutely to let her remove her false teeth, which had replaced her natural ones because of tooth decay and constant inflammation of the gums from which she had suffered since her childhood. Because this discerning husband declined to kiss a mouth without teeth, should the desire come upon him at any moment in the night, Hinna's nights were interrupted by the fear that she would swallow one of her dentures while fast asleep. But the matter which continued to arouse her hatred and resentment was her husband's insistence on having sex with her while she was completely naked, even on the coldest January nights.

The most he would concede, after much pleading, was to allow her to wear some old socks to warm her toes which became dry and withered when it was very cold.

Hinna put up with her husband's repugnant marital follies and constant harassments because she was at a loss as to what to do; moreover she was unable to speak about her problems to anyone at that time, being well aware of the first lesson of married life, that her mother had instilled in her before her marriage, which was that it was not permissible, under any circumstances, to speak about what goes on in the bedroom outside its walls, even to those who were closest to you, including your mother. For that reason, throughout her long married life, Hinna did not discuss her personal marital problems with a single soul, not even her two sisters or her mother. Instead she suffered the torment of backbiting and sarcastic comments from her daughters-in-law when they came to visit her and their eyes fell upon the red, flowered house-robe that she was wearing or the flimsy silk gown, which was really a nightgown that revealed all her arms and much of her bosom. Despite the fact that they were in the prime of youth, they were content to wear simple cotton clothes which were practical and chosen for modesty and restraint.

Once Hinna reached sixty, she began to feel rebellious in the face of these demands from her husband which never let up. A civil servant or worker usually retires when he reaches this age – everyone has the right to live in peace and tranquillity at this advanced stage of his life when he can expect to receive a government pension. Hinna desired nothing more than to be left in peace and enjoy uninterrupted sleep throughout the night, and to be able to wear clothes of her choice which made her feel comfortable without being bound by his desires summer and winter, night and day. She wanted to feel comfortable in herself and to spare the old wrinkled skin of her face from make-up. Her hands, which had recently begun to tremble, were no longer able to apply the make-up evenly as they had done in the past in order to make her face more attractive and radiant. The increasing weakness in her sight complicated the procedure and the eyeliner she applied ended up far from the inner eye lid making her look strange and comical, until the wife of her eldest son drew her attention to this and advised her to desist from using make-up altogether, particularly eyeliner. But every time she discussed the matter with her husband he refused categorically to let her abandon what he considered a necessary preparation and one of the religious rights he was entitled to from her; on one occasion when she repeated her desire to stop using make-up, he came to the conclusion that this was a kind of coquettishness and ruse in order to gain more care and attention from him. Thus he began to shower her with perfume and house clothes and all those useless feminine things like nail varnish, hand and face creams and hair oils, all of which are usually coveted by young girls still in the first flush of their married life.

One time he bought her some of her favourite walnut Turkish delight in the hope that she would yield to him in bed. But she refused this resolutely and took a firm stand without going near the mouth-watering sweets, remaining instead in her place stretched out on the sitting-room sofa on a warm winter's day. She would often point out to him that they had become grandparents to ten children, the progeny of their three sons' wives, and that it was enough to look at one of them for one's heart to overflow with happiness and joy. Would it not be more appropriate for someone of his age to draw near to God by praying and fasting and giving thanks for the happy, enjoyable years which he had lived and the abundant good health which he enjoyed and the blessed progeny he had been granted? Then she urged him to agree and behave decently, to ask God for an easy and chaste end and for a good resting place in the next world. But when the rash husband heard these words he was furious and told her that this kind of talk was wrecking his life, filling him with sadness and that it would send him to an early grave. He maintained that she was intent on denying him what he was entitled to by God; moreover she was ungrateful and unable to enjoy the blessing for which God had singled her out. For that reason she would certainly perish in hell-fire where she would suffer painful torment for her failure to obey him as God had ordained and for the way she rejected him, distancing herself from him and pursuing a path of viciousness and depravity.

Hinna however was resolute, refusing to concede to his demands to accompany him to bed, and she even began to threaten that she would take poison and kill herself if he tried to approach her. The truth was that the stength with which she refused to bow to his demands had physical causes since her body, always short and weak, had become even more so with advancing old age. She was no longer able to endure the weight of eighty-seven kilos of human bulk which is what her husband weighed at that time. When she faced him with this reality as well as everything else, his anger turned to bitter tears, and he accused her of hating him and insulting his body, calling him fat and obese when he had once been slender and strong like a bamboo stick. Then he began to lament his miserable luck at having a wife like her, with whom he had not even enjoyed a single happy day in his life, who was harsh, complicated, devoid of femininity and who should have joined a convent for life rather than marrying.

Every time Hinna became embroiled in quarrels of this sort she stood like an immovable rock refusing to go back on her resolute decision, not even weakening in the face of hot tears which were used as a new form of pressure against her. Her husband then started to complain to his sons saying that she had become an expert in tormenting him and that she had begun to neglect him and spent most of her time relaxing and sleeping. Naturally he omitted to touch on their personal relationship because, like Hinna, he had listened well to the lessons of his father on this matter. His sons would understand what was going on by reading between the lines but, in fact, they never understood what their father was on about because such concerns were far from their minds. They were barely capable of carrying out their own marital duties so far as sex was concerned because of the exhaustion they suffered, in common with most others, as users of public transport, and on account of the many other facets of everyday life which sap one's strength. They returned home, at the end of each day, so tired that they only wanted to go to bed to sleep and rest their weary bodies. Furthermore, they believed that their father's intimate life with their mother had stopped a long time ago.

After he had tried every means possible to make Hinna see reason and respond to his sexual demands, her husband at length concluded that it was pointless using peaceful methods when she slammed every door in his face. Once he had taken her to the zoo and another time to the national circus, which she had never seen in real life. Then he invited her to a meal at Hussein's but after he had tried every possible way to make himself desirable to her, he was forced to resort to harshness, particularly since she had even ignored the great efforts he made to spruce himself up by dyeing his white hair black, grooming his beard and trimming his moustache. He had even taken to spraying himself liberally, each time he went out or came in, with 'Three Fives' cologne, made from alcohol so pure that it could be used as a disinfectant. When all these attempts failed he began to curse her and fly into a rage over simple things. For instance she had the habit of putting used matches back in the box and she insisted on drinking a cordial of boiled fenugreek while she sat in bed with the bedcover over her. Even if she was at fault, she didn't deserve all these insults. It was true that he never hit her like many husbands do, but the insults he hurled at Hinna really began to hurt her feelings; they made her flare up and answer him back which she then felt unhappy about because one's husband should be respected. However, it was when he mocked her about how short she was in front of the grandchildren that she felt her resentment would overflow. Once he told them the story of a short woman who had a short broom in her short hand, who had a bed with short legs surrounded by a small mosquito net and who had a tap with a short spout. One day the woman complained to the *qadi* who was sitting amongst the people giving judgement, about flies which annoyed her and fell in the plate of honey which she had laid out for eating. All he could do was to give her a flyswatter with a long handle and say to her, "Every time you see a fly, swat it." As she sat watching him, she suddenly saw a fly settle on his great white turban; there was no alternative but to quickly lift the flyswatter and aim at his head. He was furious because she hurt him and everyone laughed at him so he ordered her to be put in the stocks to have twenty lashes on her feet so that she wouldn't do it again and would be an example to others.

One thing Hinna never imagined her husband would do was accuse her of smiling and flirting with a man – in this case the man who sold cooked *fuul* beans in the street and with whom they had dealt for ages. He told her that he was certain the man was flirting with her and that she had responded with that sweet smile which he saw spread over her face. She explained to him that the man was telling her the story of a little boy who duped him and gave him Libyan money instead of ten Egyptian pennies and that she was smiling at the boy's mischief and told the *fuul* seller to beg for compensation from God. But her husband didn't believe her and swore to cut off her hand if he caught her having any further dealings with the *fuul* seller, whatever the circumstances. Following this incident he went to the extreme lengths of buying the *fuul* every morning from a restaurant miles away from their street.

After that he completely gave up buying the Turkish delight which Hinna loved, and cut off her personal allowance, considering her a disobedient and wanton wife without compassion or mercy towards him. This made it difficult for her to buy the cheap sweets and little presents which she used to buy for her grandchildren with the little she managed to save over the month. Then, in the two years leading up to his murder, her husband tried a new tactic with Hinna which could have resulted in her expulsion from the house: he began to look for another woman.

Even though Hinna was furious about the idea of a new woman it did not bring terror to her heart as much as the idea of being thrown out of her house, within whose walls she had tasted those bitter and sweet moments for forty-five years. She had nowhere else to live, she couldn't live with any of her sons since the eldest lived in a tiny, two-roomed flat. He had two sons and two daughters and they had already turned the balcony into a third bedroom for the girls, so there was hardly enough space for his family as it was. The middle son lived with his wife in one room of his in-laws' house. His life had become hell because of this; his mother-in-law interfered in every detail of her daughter's life and always kept an eagle eye on everything that went on between her and her husband. He made great efforts not to let the mother-in-law wreck his relationship with his wife and cause a separation. As for the youngest son, his wife couldn't get on with her in-laws and the feeling was mutual. She was haughty and treated her husband with disdain because it was she who had solved the problem of finding them a place to live and paid the biggest share of the furnishings for the marital apartment from her personal savings. She also contributed the major share to the family income because she worked in a tourist hotel while her husband was only an insignificant engineer in one of the government departments. For these reasons, the possibility of Hinna going to stay with any one of her sons was completely out of the question.

THE GOLDEN CHARIOT

During the last weeks before Hinna killed her husband, she seemed rather deranged, and was consumed by anxiety since her elderly husband began to spend a great deal of time out of the house, which was uncharacteristic. When he did appear, he hardly talked to her and then only with obvious distaste, he forbade her to share his food or to sit and watch the seven o'clock serial on the television. She concluded that it didn't require much intelligence to deduce that her husband must have attached himself to another woman, and consequently the question of her remaining in the house had only become one of time. The truth was that it never occurred to Hinna, who had never studied the theory of probability because her education stopped after the fifth year of primary school, that her husband was spending the majority of his time out of the house watching blue films on a video belonging to a friend whom he met in the café, in return for little services or gifts.

However the overriding question of the other woman was enough to set Hinna's heart ablaze and shatter her nerves because she feared he would throw her out onto the street as soon as that woman arrived in the house to take her place.

One day when Hinna was emptying one of his trouser pockets before washing them, she came upon a picture of a veiled woman, whose age couldn't have been more than forty, with beautiful seductive eyes and a sensual mouth which did not need a coat of red to make it more alluring. When she looked at the picture she collapsed onto the bed still holding a decorated pin which was pricking her hand, one of the many pins she found, when turning out his pockets, which he bought from the pedlars who worked on the buses. Amongst other things, he bought cufflinks for his shirts, hair preparations and moth balls, sewing thread and elastic to tighten his underwear. He preferred to buy these from pedlars for no other reason than that he enjoyed the way they called out their wares; some told a brief tragic story before the bus started off, while some sang in the style of the well-known songs which were relayed from the enormous broadcasting building standing on the banks of the Nile, but shorter because of the lack of time available to sing them, so they were less likely to cause a headache.

This serious incident, by no means the first, meant that Hinna was forced to consider a novel solution to the tragedy that loomed ahead. Totally convinced that the other woman had become an inescapable reality, her first thought was to escape by killing herself. She found the idea of suicide difficult, however, because her soul rebelled against it and because she had done nothing to call for such an act. She came to the conclusion that there was no alternative but to get rid of her husband and put an end to the matter discreetly and, above all, without letting him find out anything about it in advance.

After Hinna had taken this important decision she felt spiritually at peace and behaved calmly with her husband, ignoring his curses as if everything was normal. It is true that she still repelled his advances but she treated him gently and showed concern for his health and affairs for fear that he might discover what she intended to do to him.

One cold winter's evening, Hinna got up to place a container full of water on the gas ring. After making quite sure she had heard his habitual snoring which resembled the croaking of a frog and which satisfied her that he was in a deep sleep, she opened the gas cylinder fully, made sure the windows of the apartment were firmly shut, then slipped out to spend the remainder of the night on the sitting-room balcony. She wrapped herself in a blanket and sat with her back leaning against the door, which she had locked from the outside, making sure that it wouldn't open and allow any air to enter the apartment. She remained in this position all night until daybreak.

As has been said before, the police did not believe that her husband had died by fate and divine decree through asphyxiation because, when they arrived at the apartment – immediately after the urgent call from Hinna's neighbours who heard her screaming and slapping her face – she appeared to be in perfect health and showed no signs of weakness or breathlessness. Instead she seemed perfectly composed and the police could find nothing wrong with her except that she coughed every now and then. What they did not know, of course, was that she did so because she had spent the entire night outside in the cold. She was, however, also crying quite genuinely because she was upset at losing a friend who had been her companion for forty-five years. When, at the enquiry, the prosecution faced her with the obvious discrepancy between the good state of her own health and her husband's death by suffocation, despite the fact that she was in the same house when the incident occurred, Hinna claimed that she had spent the night in question in the sitting-room – which was far from the kitchen – because her continual coughing was disturbing the deceased. The police would have believed this story, had the prosecution not discovered a foolish mistake on Hinna's part. This was to have left the taps of two gas burners open instead of only the one beneath the pot of water. She had been anxious to let as much gas as possible escape in order to cause death in the shortest time, in case her husband woke up and noticed the smell of gas spreading in the house.

After that it was easy to bring a charge of premeditated murder against Hinna and to find plenty of other evidence to support it – the gas taps were only the obvious clue. But Hinna continued to stick to her original statement, and would not deviate from it despite the fact that she was bombarded by questions. The curious thing was that she seemed to believe her story completely and became enraged every time the prosecution mentioned the word murder; it was as if she were being accused of something she had never done. In this way, during the whole period of her investigation and trial, she remained extremely irate at what she considered gross injustice. She was angry with the prosecution whose representative persistently exaggerated the accusations against her, insisting that she was an evil old beast who had devoured her benefactor and the person closest to her, violating all the laws of morality and the godly laws which were ordained by all religions.

As soon as the judgement was announced Hinna felt relief from the burden which was weighing heavily upon her. From behind bars, she set out to dispel the alarm of her sons, who had burst into tears, reassuring them that she would be all right. She even started advising them about the supplies they should bring her when they visited her in prison which included some of her favourite Turkish delight, a crochet needle and some cotton upholstery thread.

Hinna experienced the first moment of real happiness since she killed her husband when she was installed in the ward for the weak with other old women; she regarded it as a place of refuge for the remaining years of her life, convinced that she would be dead before the ten-year sentence was up. But this did not stop her sometimes dreaming of a better life should she live to see through her period in prison. She revelled in dreams of reorganizing the furniture in her apartment according to her taste, rather than her husband's. She also thought of renting out the room he died in – the biggest room in the place – to one or two female students. Her neighbour on the floor below had also rented out to some of those students who came up from the provinces to study at university. She would eat the food of her choice and would start cooking spinach again which she had given up because it was bad for her husband's mild kidney complaint. She would even buy a new quilt instead of that old one which was worn out and whose history went back to the early days of their marriage – the quilt whose lining she had so often begged her husband to renew.

Meanwhile, Aziza was making a different plan for Hinna, the most beautiful and grandiose plan among small earthly plans, which was that she would accompany her to heaven, and would include her in the golden chariot with its magic, white, winged horses, which would take off to the sound of rousing melodies provided by the god of music and entertainment, like those she heard an army band play long ago in the city. And when the chariot ascended, riding gracefully on the clouds, perhaps Hinna would forget the spinach and the quilt and the husband who killed her a thousand times during forty-five years while she only killed him once. She would then know how much Aziza loved and valued her because she enabled her to obtain the happiness and blessing which she deserved as one of those unfortunate women in the women's prison. Moreover, she would seat her next to Azima, 'the giant', who was the tallest and noblest woman Aziza had known throughout the period of her imprisonment.

Anyone who set eyes on Azima, the giant, would have been shocked by her strange appearance. Even the head of the women's prison was astonished when he took responsibility for her as an inmate of the prison and saw her for the first time; in fact he abandoned the customary reticence of an official in his position and began to ask her about the secret of her amazing height.

Naturally Azima did not give a clear answer, because she never knew the secret of her awesome height; she was over two metres tall – heads taller than other women – and even quarter of a metre taller than her father, who was considered tall.

Until Azima was twelve, she was a normal child who seemed slightly tall in comparison to her peers but not remarkably so, nor in a way which caused alarm to her family who were preparing her for marriage like her older sisters, like any ordinary young girl looking ahead to the day she would find a suitable match. When Azima failed to obtain her primary certificate – quite usual for most pupils at this stage, given the state of the schools – she became free to complete her education in domestic affairs considered a priority in grooming girls for marriage.

However not long after this signs of Azima's problem appeared. She began to shoot up with startling speed, made more obvious by her remarkable thinness and the lack of proportion in her physique: her lower half was extended in contrast with the short upper half and her long neck ended in a small head with big, rather bulging eyes so that when you looked at her you thought she might be a giraffe in a human form. By the time she turned sixteen, she had grown so much that she seemed far taller than any other human being around, and was exposed to a great deal of ridicule in the street and even at home; this put a severe strain on her just as it would on any adolescent girl who wanted to be loved and accepted by people generally, and by the opposite sex in particular. She began to feel so bitter that she attempted suicide but her attempt failed because when she threw herself from the balcony of her home, which was on the fourth floor in a block of flats, she fell unexpectedly onto a cement cart which was crossing the road. She suffered nothing more than a broken front tooth which she banged against the metal edge of the vehicle as it proceeded, carrying her with it to the end of the street. The broken tooth was a lasting memorial to this abortive attempt.

If this incident did not scar Azima, another was to change the course of her life completely. A few months later an uncle of hers died in the flower of his youth. It was a tragic death which shook everyone who heard about it. One night, out of the blue, the building where he lived began to fall down. After he had saved his mother, father and his three sisters from certain death, a neighbour asked him to help save her paralyzed mother. He rushed to carry the old woman, who had crawled out to one of the balconies, and threw her down to the crowd which was waiting to catch her below. However, after the woman was saved, a huge piece of stone fell on the young man and squashed him flat.

Then the quarter in which the event took place witnessed a funeral ceremony of the kind which had not taken place since the funeral of the martyrs of the 1919 Revolution, when the people clubbed together to set up the biggest mourning tent possible and hired the best man they could afford to recite the Qur'an. A large crowd paid their respects at his final resting place at the end of an amazing funeral procession which everyone joined in and brought the traffic to a halt for half an hour in Mohamed Ali street, leading to the Citadel. The traffic jam lasted two hours, even after the funeral procession was over. The cars had edged onto the old tramway undeterred by the soldier in charge of the traffic, who hadn't eaten anything from dawn till the afternoon of the funeral, and now was too busy eating bread stuffed with *falafel* to notice.

After the members of the funeral procession had paid their last respects, the women grouped together in the small square in front of the house of the recently bereaved family, which was none other than Azima's family home. Inside, there were enough tears flowing to cause another death by drowning. In the agitation and emotion of the occasion several women fainted through the enormous effort they had expended screaming and slapping their faces. Amongst them was the mother of the dead man and the fiancée whose hopes had been dashed and was left mourning with her intended mother-in-law.

At that time Azima's talents as a female mourner blossomed in a new way. She was able to deliver words of immense consolation to those who mourned in verses full of pun, antithesis, simile and metaphor and other rhetorical devices emerging from the rich resources of her newly-discovered imagination and her poetic inspiration, the extent of which matched her bodily height.

In addition to the heroic role he had played, the man they had buried a short time ago was also extremely handsome; this enabled Azima to eulogize and make much of his physical attributes. This served to intensify the grief of the fiancée who abandoned any hope of becoming engaged to a man like him again.

From that day, Azima became the official mourner of the quarter and after a time her activities spread to other surrounding quarters. She could be found on the spot at any calamity which afflicted a family. Through this activity Azima discovered a vocation which enabled her to come to terms with her life, which had always previously been full of psychological pressures of a kind difficult for any young girl to bear. She had suffered continual mockery, directed particularly towards her height which did not conform to the accepted standards of femininity; from time immemorial these have decreed that a woman's height should correspond to her designated role in society.

As a result of such prevailing standards, Azima's family were convinced that her desperate wish to marry – an obsession which had gripped Azima's heart for many a long day – was an impossible dream. As a result of this, she decided to dedicate her life to the world of mourning, thereby finding fulfilment and making a place for herself in society. The gravity of her new role meant that she had to adopt a correspondingly dignified appearance. She made sure that when she went out she wore long, black clothes which suited her because they hid her hugely long legs from view; similarly she began to be seen everywhere with a veil of light chiffon on her head, which she tied in place with a piece of black artificial silk. The only womanly adornment which Azima retained was black kohl on her eyelids which she put on as soon as she woke in the morning and had washed her face; this enhanced the size of her sad expressive eyes, which seemed to belong to someone created only for sorrow and pain.

As time passed, Azima discovered she had amazing skills in her field and could produce an elegy to suit the particular qualities of the deceased which she delivered on request for the bereaved relatives. She even managed to versify details of his age, the circumstances surrounding the death and the bodily appearance of the deceased in a harmonious way: if he was tall and broad, like Anwar Majdi in those films of the forties and fifties, then the verse would reflect this and say: "The earth holds his height in her perpetual might" or if he was thin and delicate she would say: "The cruel jaws of death have snatched away this little sparrow's breath". She improvised and excelled in her delivery if the deceased was a young man or a beautiful woman who was still a virgin – or at least a virgin according to the official marriage records of the district. She moved the hearts of those who listened and made them explode with grief. The impact was intensified through the words in the poem which she used to rhapsodize about sadness to such effect that she sometimes encountered problems with the bereaved family. On one occasion the brother of one of those being mourned threatened to hit her if she didn't cease her lamentation and leave immediately because the burden of emotion and sorrow that his mother felt for her dead son had reached such a pitch that she had suffered a serious heart attack. The flame of all this grief had been kindled by the lamentations and elaboration which Azima delivered so passionately in the *rajaz* metre at the ceremony to commemorate the anniversary of his death.

In addition to this, and to perfect her role which was beginning to earn her enough to make a living, Azima began to study religious exhortations and sermons which she delivered at funeral ceremonies. She flawlessly memorized the *Surat al-Rahman* [the Merciful] as well as some shorter *suras* of the Qur'an which had lodged in her memory since her primary school days and she delivered them in a voice which she tried to make as full as possible, not an easy task with a voice box unsuited to the demands of her intensely inspirational style of singing. In her leisure hours she would soothe her voice with aniseed or ginger which the family of the deceased would offer her, or sit at the lunch table to eat boiled meat or a dish of sopped bread, meat and broth. She had also started to interpret dreams, according to the methodology of Ibn Sirin, but changing them radically since she invented happy endings which pleased and relieved the bereaved relatives.

The existence of cassettes with *suras* recorded by well-known readers of the Qur'an accredited by Al-Azhar did not present any real competition to her nor did she fear the Islamic associations who forbade these ceremonies of lamentation and elegy because they considered them contradictory to orthodox religious education. Lately these ceremonies had become more popular for reasons she never knew, but she suspected they responded to a need for something which had been lost through the empty words sung by the poets which inundated the public day and night on the radio and television. Equally, those obscure poems written by poets who fancied themselves as avant-garde writers and which were occasionally published in magazines and newspapers did not in any way address the issues and sentiments which preoccupy the public. Nor did poems by the other outmoded poets who insisted on writing in the old Amudi style, weaving their poetry from worn out threads of a chivalry which no longer existed, for the values of the noble knight were no longer suited to the trials of daily life and the bitter struggle for survival.

Some years later, when her undoubted mastery as an official mourner was famed, Azima started investing her money in a new way, secured around her neck rather than in the bank: that is, she transferred her earnings from money into gold jewellery. She also began to participate in the Saints' day festivals with religious poems and poems of praise which were well received and broadcast with the help of modern technology – namely the microphone – capable of giving strength, magic and brilliance to weak voices. Azima's voice was not particularly distinguished, but because everyone seemed to have taken up singing, not only on Saints' days but also on radio, television and on the cassettes which had spread like wildfire from the furthermost point in the north of the country to the lowest point in the south, Azima was able to enter the musical arena through a door which was wide open and found herself amongst a public who loved singing. This opening was through the medium of *mawal*, religious verses, a field in which she became highly proficient. She strove to produce a voice, strengthened by electronic means, which was as powerful as possible, taking advantage of the hoarseness which followed from long years of being a professional mourner and which won her the amazement of all who gathered to listen to her during the festivals. She was driven to swallow quantities of various drugs to produce the sad, rasping quality of her voice, which expressed deep-seated emotions of dejection and shattered hopes – hopes which were at the mercy of eternal fate and which were elevated beyond the continuous misery most people endure.

Hardly a year had passed before Azima had her own music group to accompany her during the nights of the famous Saints' days of Cairo like Hussein and Sayyida Zaynab and Sayyid El-Badawi in Tanta. Her repertoire had expanded as she responded to her increased popularity as the prime singer of *mawal*. Her verses were recorded on cassettes with her picture on the cover, smiling broadly, and which did not show the three gold crowns in her mouth. Above the picture was her name and below it: "The Leading Professional Singer of *Mawal*". This was the grand title she gave herself like the other grandiose titles people frequently gave themselves in all other walks of life. Azima won the adulation of the masses through her cassettes because of the clear descriptions of love and passion in her poetry, which also had religious overtones in praise of the famous Prophet and his blessed family. In this way she followed in the footsteps of all the popular eulogists who emulated the greatest and most erudite Sufis of the Middle Ages. Azima often incorporated selections into her poems – slightly altered – from the great Sufi poets like Ibn El-Farid, whose mosque on the Muqattam Hills she had often visited in order to offer prayers and blessings. She also used the poems of Ibn El-Arabi, Dhi El-Nun El-Nasri and others who were part of a sect who had experienced the divine light and had attained a special position close to God. Azima got hold of some cheap, popular copies of these poems from the booksellers, in Hussein or Sayyida Zaynab Square, who spread their wares on the pavements.

Azima's artistic activities required her to change out of her usual black mourning clothes into fine clothes of coloured silk embossed with pearls and gold and silver spangles, with a veil to match the colour of her dress and a head band embroidered with gold or silver thread to match her wealth. Then she discovered that blue powdered kohl, widely used amongst the peasant women of the Delta, suited her better than the lampblack which she had been using. All this adornment was for the sake of her adoring public before whom she wanted to appear as beautiful as her physique would allow. She gradually began to give up her lamenting activities not only because of her new public but because she had spent enough of her youth being sad. She then stopped going to funerals except in extremely rare cases when the financial return was worth the strain of all this misfortune and sadness.

However a third event came to play a part in Azima the giant's life which was to change her destiny completely. Her talents would probably have been sufficient for her to become a popular artist like Zekriyya El-Hegawi, or she might have joined those popular folk singers who spring up on stage like wild mushrooms, promoted by the Government which wants to be seen to be preserving popular culture.

Her tragedy was not one of those simple events which pass through the life of a talented poet – she had not lived in a time like that of the famous Greek poet Sappho – but her talents emerged in an age which places culture at the bottom of its list so that the word itself has been virtually erased from the dictionary. After Azima reached forty, something happened which had never happened before: she became entangled in a love affair like a dove which learns to fly for the first time and falls prey to a skilled hunter. It involved a member of her music group who affected her entire being and inspired her soul with his passionate poems, which drove people wild. The poems were dedicated to Sayyid Hussein and if they made none of the customary references to other members of the Holy Prophet's family it was almost certainly to underline the fact that the name of the feckless suitor was also Hussein. He was not very skilled on the flute and had originally joined her group as a player of the one-stringed fiddle. But he got his job after they failed to find a good flautist because most of the musicians preferred to work with groups in the Pyramids Road or the city night clubs rather than join popular groups whose work was tied to the seasons of the saints' festivals and the feast days.

This Hussein was one of those men who know how to put their hand on a woman's shoulder, and once he had scrutinized Azima's body and was convinced that she was worth a considerable amount of money in addition to the plentiful gold dangling on her arms, around her neck and from her ears, he began to cast mad passionate glances in her direction. Prompted by his many experiences in love, he identified her as a woman who desperately desired a man, whose thirsty body needed to be quenched and whose soul was full of emotions seeking to be fulfilled with love and beauty.

Azima's lover not only awakened her soul but also activated her body, which began to fill out for the first time. It must be admitted that she had begun to resemble an enemy barricade – like one of those mud brick walls used for fortification which were set up at the entrance of buildings during each war which our army fought against Israel. But her appearance, in any case, seemed better when she turned around, since her face had filled out making her wide nose less prominent. What had always seemed an impossible dream at last became a reality when she heard tender words of love for the first time from a man. Azima gave bountifully to her lover, giving all a resourceful woman could give to the man she loved. This began with the money she earned through her artistic activities amassed from the pockets of her admirers, peasants from distant country villages and the poor of the city who made pilgrimages to hear her sing, and it ended with her giving him her huge, unfeminine body.

Not long passed before the flautist became lord of her soul and lord of the music group too, after demoting the first flute to second place. In the end the lover, who was a clever opportunist, took charge of her affairs taking decisions over every aspect of her life and gaining absolute authority and power over her.

Azima's love for this man was such that she could balance these factors in her mind and was prepared to sacrifice her money and her soul – in fact all that she possessed in the world – for this "pocket" of a man waiting to be filled, whom fate had bestowed upon her, on one condition – that he marry her. In this way she hoped to find the true protection which would come from a legalized relationship with Hussein, this catch, whose children she was hoping to bear. When she explained her position to him plainly, confident that the idea of marriage would not be an imposition but would make him happy and full of good intentions, she was surprised when he evaded her question. She never realized that the flautist, who knew all about the inner workings of women's hearts, had come to the conclusion that the best way of keeping a woman's heart was to avoid marrying her; thus he refused her offer which had not come as a surprise. He received the proposal extremely calmly one morning while sitting next to her on the comfortable sofa in her sitting room, drinking coffee and smoking their usual morning water pipe together. He told her, as he fondled her long fingers with filed nails, painted with light red varnish, that his love for her knew no bounds and that he was passsionate about every bit of her beautiful body, especially her long white neck which was plump as a silver jar, but that he could never marry her in his present circumstances. He was employed by her and would be unable to meet the necessary costs of a wedding and of a marital home. For that reason he would rather postpone marriage until his financial circumstances improved when he would be a worthy suitor and could marry her openly and unashamedly before God and the Prophet, for all the world to see.

At this point in the conversation, Azima was greatly moved and her heart beat furiously since she believed that he was being sincere about everything he said to her. While he spoke he fixed his eyes on hers with a look of inflamed love which melted her heart and aroused her feelings more and more. For that reason she accepted what he said and then proposed that she sell a giant gilded copy of the Qur'an (weighing the same as eleven solid gold bracelets) which she had bought several years ago for about five thousand pounds and whose value had probably increased by two thousand. So that they might become engaged, she would give him the money she obtained from this sale to offer her as a dowry. But the flute player, who was watching her face as she spoke, and particularly her gleaming gold molars, was secretly ensuring that he did not fall into the dangerous trap and did not become hemmed in without hope of escape. He swore by Almighty God three times and begged Him with raised hands to burn him in hell-fire until he was turned into pieces of charcoal like those on the water pipe which burned in front of him, should he ever stretch out his hand and take money from her or further any step towards marriage with her which was not done with money earned by the sweat of his brow, dripping naturally, from the exertion of blowing the flute.

Azima found it difficult to swallow the feeble pretexts of her hypocritical lover because they were inconsistent. Until now he had been taking money from her whenever he wanted and willingly accepting any gift she offered which enabled him to maintain a slick image. This might be the cash which she slipped into his hand from time to time or the Mercedes which she bought and placed at his disposal whenever he wanted it. The reality of the situation was that his excuses were meaningless for, even if he laid eggs like a hen in a coop for a hundred years he would never be able to collect the necessary money to marry her, since he had absolutely nothing.

Full of hurt pride, Azima decided to withdraw from a relationship which, as far as she was concerned, could never continue illicitly. She was beginning to get a bad reputation and people were giving her dirty looks. She made do with barricading her great love behind the door of her heart with a bolt and key so that it should remain locked inside, bursting with memories of beautiful days of passion which had passed through her life like a dream, from which she had awakened quickly and whose progression towards a happy end had been disrupted. The flute player, however, did not accept this break in their relationship and began to play on her emotions again, redoubling his words of love and his passionate glances. Although she felt her feelings soften, she insisted on remaining resolute before him and stuck to her decision to break with him since legal marriage was the condition she made, first and foremost, for continuing the relationship. On this basis she refused the new offer he made her of marriage without contract which provided for no legal commitment. She persisted in her view that he should not disregard the legal sanctity of marriage any more than the fickle Government should ignore its pledges to the poor. Azima, on the contrary, reduced her relationship with the flute player to the minimum, restricting it simply to work. She could not actually do without him because of the lack of players in the music market but she managed to withstand the emotional pressure from her faithless lover and to avert her face from him, despite the fact that her heart at that time could have done with ten of Farid El-Atrash's tear-jerking songs to help her mourn her severed passion and her miserable luck in the world of love. However, when the expert lover failed to resolve the matter peacefully he became impatient with the stale-mate and he began to reveal his other, evil side. He started spreading rumours about the details of his relationship with her, in a most despicable way, insinuating all kinds of things which he left to people's fertile imaginations. His aim in this was to make Azima submit to him through her desperation to retrieve the scattered details of her love and to make her buy his silence.

Azima considered this way of carrying on as crude – no better than a hyena who can't resist tearing the meat of its dead prey to pieces – which is what she considered herself to be after her hopes in him had been shattered. She began to fume with rage, a sentiment shared by the musician who was the first fiddler in her group and a real friend to her. He had become her right hand man in her artistic affairs as well as personal matters, even after she fell in love, because he had absolute faith in her as the best popular singer of mourning songs of her time, after the death of the master of mourning songs, Mohamed Abdel Matalib. This view was partly based on his ability as a fiddler descended from an ancient family of itinerant musicians who sang popular songs and whose profession had been handed down as far as four generations back.

Azima's burning anger revealed itself through a small plan of revenge to be inflicted on the perpetrator of treachery. She decided to hire one of the experts who practised various forms of permanent bodily disablement for the beggars who frequented the area around the Al-Hussein mosque and served the rest of the beggars in Cairo, to carry out the castration of her former lover. One evening, after she made him believe that her deep love would resume as before, she lured him to the first fiddle player's house in the Tarb area for a practice session with the rest of the group in preparation for the coming festival of Sayyida Zaynab. Azima rehearsed her voice and sang a new song of praise to the Prophet, peace be upon Him, over and over again until she sang it well. It was originally a love song by Faiza Ahmed, which Mohamed Abdel Wahhab had put to music for her a long time ago, but Azima changed the words to suit the occasion and to make it a vehicle of praise to the Prophet. Meanwhile she kept to the melody played by the group with a small alteration in keeping with the popular mood of frenzy, customary at saints' festivals. Most of the playing was given over to the popular percussion instruments and the strings, traditionally confined to the one-stringed fiddle which countered with a tuneful melody while Azima's husky voice sang the words: "My heart yearns for you."

After they had finished rehearsing, all the members of the group left the house except for Azima and the flautist. He sat down next to her to listen to her words of repentance and request for his pardon after he was assured of his success in awakening her heart to his renewed calls of love. But it was not long before he fell into a deep swoon after numerous glasses of rosé wine which had been heavily drugged. When it was certain that he was unconscious he was quickly moved to the large room which belonged to the first fiddle. Here the castration expert awaited him, in whose veins flowed an ancient gift handed down through the blood of his fathers from the time of the Mamluks. He stood up after he had confirmed his faith in God and the Prophet, rolled up his sleeves and checked that the effect of the drugs had not worn off. Then he made sure that his surgical tools were properly sterilized in a little aluminium vessel of boiling water on a black stove of the kind usually used to prepare coffee; he found the cotton and muslin, tincture of iodine and enough ground sulphonamide which he placed in the boiling water. Then without flinching at the fierce heat, he extracted a straight razor made from the kind of steel which barbers usually use and used it to cut off what was to earn him five thousand pounds, half of it paid in advance. Once the operation was successfully completed and some iodine and sulphonomide had been applied with bandages of cotton and muslin, the flautist was quickly moved to his house, the key to which Azima had kept since before they first split up, and placed on his bed. He was covered with blankets and left to himself until the dawning of the new day when he would awaken from his drugged sleep transformed into a handsome eunuch.

The first fiddle tried to take the place of the lover whose treachery had been so recently avenged and offered to marry her immediately, despite the fact that he was already married with children. But Azima considered his offer as a form of pity for her and an attempt to restore her damaged self-esteem and even to silence people's accusations against her. She rejected his request tactfully for these noble reasons and for other reasons not so noble. The first was that the first fiddle was conspicuously short which meant that he hardly came up to her waist and secondly she was still in love with the flute player despite the fact that he was a lost cause. He was the lover whose beautiful memory she wanted to preserve without thinking about another man, or embarking upon marriage. Indeed her hopes in men generally were shattered and she considered what had happened as a lesson to her and an experience which had alerted her to the fact that she had been enticed by fame and money and had thought she was able to buy love just as she bought anything else from the souk.

Thereafter, life for Azima might almost have reverted to how it was before the flautist entered her life, had he not resolved to avenge himself for the hellish operation which had targeted his most cherished possession. After he discovered what had happened to him he chose to remain silent because he did not want to be the subject of mockery, particularly from those to whom he had divulged the secrets of his love affair with Azima. He decided not to complain to the police or involve them in this disaster, preferring to deal with it in his own way in order to save time: a day is like a year with the authorities, and the police would draw the whole thing out transferring the matter to the prosecution and the court. This would have meant him harbouring a sense of burning hatred for a long time, perhaps for years. For that reason he decided to exercise his right to revenge on his own and to deal with the matter in hand in stages. The first step concentrated on the first fiddle in his capacity as the mastermind of the castration operation and the second concerned Azima for whom he would slowly prepare a dish of revenge on a gentle heat until it was ready to be eaten; the first ingredient would be to fling concentrated sulphuric acid over Azima's face to disfigure her so badly that her artistic future would be ruined. She would be unable, after that, to stand before her beloved audience with a horrific face, she would like the frightening man with the skinless leg with whom his mother used to threaten him when he was small in order to get him to go to bed. After that he would make her kneel down in front of him and make her crawl towards him on all fours, after forcing her to eat the dust which he had trodden on; he would make her beg for forgiveness and mercy.

However, the flautist's plan failed at its first stage when the attempt of the hired murderers to kill the first fiddle merely left him badly wounded. This occasioned his urgent removal to the Hussein University Hospital, with the police investigating the matter accompanying him. Although the victim did not accuse Hussein the flautist, nevertheless he identified his attackers. They had tried to kill him as he walked through the cemetery on his way back from visiting Azima in her home in Bab Al-Shaariyya where he had been sorting out the wages for the new fiddle players who had joined the group, one of whom was a young student from the Arab Institute of Music.

At the investigation the failed assassins acknowledged, after each received a slap on the face by way of opening the investigation, that they carried out this attempt on the instructions of Hussein the flautist, who was to pay them a thousand pounds to be shared as they agreed. When Hussein was called up before the prosecution, he confessed that he had instigated this plot as an act of revenge, and they ordered a medical examination which established that he really had been castrated a short time ago. The finger of suspicion then pointed at Azima after she decided to absolve the first fiddle from their line of enquiry, and swore that he had nothing to do with setting up the flautist's castration either directly or indirectly. She was desperate that the group should go on and that there should be someone to look after its interests with loyalty and devotion. The court found her guilty of the offence of grievous bodily harm for which a financial penalty was insufficient. They sentenced her to imprisonment and a fine of twenty-five thousand pounds, of which Azima did not pay a penny, preferring to spend the necessary years in prison after handing all her jewellery to the first fiddle for safe-keeping as a security for the future when she finally got out.

Azima faced up to the years in prison with patience and resignation, she considered it as simply the penalty she paid for having dedicated herself to her great love; indeed she was even prepared to face death on his behalf. She lived in prison with her beautiful memories of Hussein the flautist, which were constantly with her, those memories which made her soul overflow with all of that love which had come to her by chance. Her only consolation in the long days and nights in the prison, which time forgets, were the old songs of Umm Kalsoum which kindled the fire in her heart, in which the spark of love had not been extinguished, the songs she never tired of repeating all the time she was alone with herself at night. These were songs which made Aziza review the nature of Azima, after finding her distasteful and irritating. She had believed her to be a demon, who sprang from the earth, who did not even belong to the human race and had lost her way, ending up in prison, when her real place was in some old pit. But hearing the humanity in Azima's voice which had been suppressed as far as her public was concerned but which often still intoned those wonderful songs of Umm Kalsoum, Aziza discovered her true value, nobility and decency as someone who could only be a real angel.

For that reason, Aziza decided to seat Azima next to Hinna in the golden chariot. A measure of Azima's nobility manifested itself in her sympathy towards the wretched Hinna, especially when Hinna was continually ill for a period of two weeks, confining her to bed. Azima waited on her like a daughter would wait on a mother, even carrying her to the toilet to see to her needs, and returning her to bed in the ward for the weak after washing her. She spent ages coaxing her to eat which required a great deal of patience; Hinna had been refusing to eat the awful black prison bread because her false teeth had begun to work loose in her mouth after losing so much weight and becoming much weaker. Azima soaked the bread in water and broke it into little pieces and fed it to her while singing cheerful songs which brought a smile to Hinna's lips.

In addition Azima was a wonderful performer and the passengers in the chariot might need some singing to entertain them on their long heavenly journey. This meant including Azima, which was exactly what Aziza resolved should happen.

Aziza informed Azima of the important and secret decision in two words, and no more, while they were washing their faces one morning in the bathroom. Azima gave Aziza a friendly morning greeting while she was scrubbing her face with soap which meant that she did not notice the silent nod with which Aziza replied, only hearing her voice mingled with the splashing water coming from the tap, without understanding what she meant by the words:

"Get set!"

3

The Cow Goddess Hathur

It took no time at all – not even the time it took to soft boil an egg – for Aziza to decide that there was one person who simply must be included on the voyage to heaven. This was the peasant woman, Umm El-Khayr, for whom Aziza felt a warmth which was close to love. Ever since she first saw her in the prison, Aziza had clung to Umm El-Khayr and unburdened her heart to her. She first saw her squatting, with her sleeves rolled up, crumbling bits of bread into a blue tin dish onto which she poured a little powdered milk and water to give to the favourite prison cat. It had just put down four kittens with tightly shut eyes after a difficult birth which lasted the whole night. Two of them had inherited features from the unknown father, since they were dark grey streaked with black, unlike their mother, who was the colour of a ripe apricot and so known as "Mishmisha" by the prisoners.

At this moment, Aziza was leaning against the edge of the window of the geriatric ward overlooking the long corridor which led into the rest of the wards. She smiled to Umm El-Khayr and said: "God give you strength!" Then she watched Mishmisha lap up the bread and milk in the dish and added: "Praise be to God, little Mishmisha, God willing they will grow up in your glory."

Umm El-Khayr's lips parted to reveal beautiful old teeth, rarely found in a sixty-five year old peasant woman. She spoke as if Mishmisha was a real woman who had suffered greatly giving birth: "D'you know love, I didn't sleep a wink all night because of her – I felt the pain rip me apart as if I was going through it myself. I pleaded with God to let the birth go peacefully then daybreak proclaimed the glory of God and the first kitten came out."

Umm El-Khayr invited Aziza into the ward to drink some tea with her, tempting her by adding a little dried milk from the tin her middle son had brought her on his last visit a few days ago. He knew that his mother was fond of milk with her tea and she would always tell them, when she saw them drinking it black, that they should add milk to dilute the poison.

Aziza sat next to Umm El-Khayr to drink the milky tea and to gain access to Umm El-Khayr's heart whose openness and generosity made her the most eligible person to make the voyage to heaven. She sat, mesmerized, and listened to her story without showing the slightest trace of boredom despite the traditional peasant style which characterized her narration. It was a slow process which involved repetition, additions and embellishments full of description and simile and a great deal of darting from one story to another. But Aziza who was perpetually peevish in prison, did not find Umm El-Khayr irritating and found no cause to despise her. Nor did her origins – which were inescapably those of a peasant – arouse Aziza's scorn despite the fact that she herself came from an old city family who looked upon peasants as boorish, coarse and dirty with an unbearable smell like that of Sabiha who used to come from the country to sell butter and cheese to Aziza's family. Sabiha would stay overnight with them to boil and clarify the butter into ghee in those far off days when her mother would store nearly fifty kilograms of ghee each year in the huge clay pot which was lost, amongst all the other things in the house, during the fire. But Aziza had noticed another, strange, elusive smell which was not the coarse peasant smell of dung. She remembered smelling the rancid odour coming from Sabiha when she annointed her hair with her dirty fingers covered in butter after she had finished weighing it out – all in an attempt to soften her dishevelled locks and to refine her appearance a little. But now Aziza thought about the strange smell which distinguished Umm El-Khayr from any other woman in the prison, and she guessed that it strongly resembled the smell of suckling babies – that is the smell of milk mixed with an innocence, gentleness and frailty. Perhaps its unusual combination accounted for her fascination with this smell in the same way that she had been captivated by the perfume her stepfather would sometimes secretly give her in that beautiful past. Aziza had never experienced this baby smell before because she had never been a mother. She had been unaware of the beauty of motherhood until she came to prison and witnessed the mothers' thirst for their little ones and watched those little wretches who were sentenced to suck from the breast of their mothers behind the high prison walls until they were weaned.

Perhaps one of the extremely limited benefits of prison was that the seclusion imposed long periods of contemplation and the possibility of discovering aspects of life which were inaccessible to all but those who had tasted the bitterness of banishment. The forced isolation within the boundaries of the prison walls separated them from all the daily trivialities of life in the vast ocean of humanity.

Aziza's enthusiasm for Umm El-Khayr was such that she was determined to seat her next to herself in the front of the chariot, which was a pretty compassionate decision bearing in mind what had happened between the peasant woman and young Aida. Aziza informed her of her decision when she was sitting alone in her cell sipping her mock wine and smoking. She fetched another glass for Umm El-Khayr so that they could drink a toast to the heavenly ascent together and to her honoured place in the golden chariot, but Umm El-Khayr never lifted her glass, just as she never heard Aziza announce her important decision because, at that time she was busy in the ward for the elderly adjoining Aziza's ward on the right, cradling and rocking the little girl belonging to Halima, the warder. At this moment the child was nestling against her huge milk-coloured breasts, as dry of milk as the breasts of any woman aged over sixty-five – not yet even a year old, she was unable to suck her natural mother's milk which had dried up over the years. Instead she was comforted by the tenderness and old country songs, lodged in the recesses of this old peasant's memory, that poured forth as a reminder of all the love Umm El-Khayr had given to her ten children, whose four children she had in turn raised, giving a helping hand to their mothers. Her married life had begun only six months after the red sign of puberty had first appeared to announce the readiness of her female apparatus for the task of pregnancy and childbirth, and these ten children were the surviving fruit of fifteen confinements.

Umm El-Khayr did not hear Aziza's secret decision about the ascent to heaven, since her mind was completely taken up with happy thoughts about her children: her eldest son was successfully investing his money in new land to add to his existing property while the youngest was working hard to get into university; she thought about her son who had gone into the army and her daughters who were all happily married. If any of them came to her complaining of their husbands, she would ensure that she soon returned to the marital nest, reinforced and with peace of mind restored. Her heart beat furiously and the blood rushed to her head each time she thought of her fourth son and imagined that he might have been in this dreadful place instead of her, sleeping as she did now on the rotten foam rubber mattress on which so many others had been fated to sleep. She begged protection from the Devil and praised God as she imagined how her son would have been forced to eat the awful food and scraps which she was offered in prison. The horror of what he was spared was made more vivid by the sight of the black iron bars at which she was forced to gaze and which gripped her tortured soul.

Her voice broke into a trembling song to the suckling infant, lying contentedly in her lap. She praised God because she had been able to spare her son, the apple of her eye, from twenty-five years in prison which was the sentence she received for a drug offence which always carries the maximum sentence. When the police raided the house she rushed to the scene and took responsibility for all the drugs they had discovered, hidden in the large basket kept for rice which stood by the oven, thereby absolving her son from the whole affair.

She felt such joy fill her heart as she remembered her success in saving her beloved son that she lifted the little prison baby onto her lap and began to kiss her tenderly, effusively. Then she threw her gently into the air and brought her down again and the baby, who was delighted with these amusing acrobatics, opened her mouth wide with what seemed to be a smile. Umm El-Khayr left off playing with the child and her strong voice, which had so often broken into song at weddings in her rural village, fell silent following shouts from Lula the hair stylist which were raised in objection to the din she was making with the warden's baby. The baby's mother often left her child to spend the night with Umm El-Khayr to save bringing her to the prison every morning. Her home was more than an hour away on public transport which, in the morning rush-hour, was crammed full of passengers in an inhuman way. At this moment Lula was busy looking at her stars in the paper as Umm abdul-Aziz, who was reputed to be able to see into the future, wanted to sleep and had refused to read her palm.

Aziza stayed awake throughout that night thinking about Umm El-Khayr and marvelled at the abundant vigour and good health of her body, despite all the children she had given birth to year after year. She was the only inmate in the ward for the old and disabled who did not suffer from high blood pressure and whose heart remained completely healthy, as confirmed by the prison doctor who had examined her. Her eyesight was so strong that she was able to extract a tiny piece of glass, hardly visible to the naked eye, from Aziza's fingertip using a pair of eyebrow tweezers. This happened when the window pane in the surgery broke one day and even though Aziza removed the largest piece of glass she didn't realize as she rested her hand on the ledge that it was still full of little pieces which were difficult to see.

What amazed Aziza about Umm El-Khayr more than anything was the incredibly high morale she maintained most of the time, as well as her peace of mind and composure which made her virtually the only prisoner Aziza had seen during her long stay in prison who was not addicted to smoking, and drinking tea, which she only drank occasionally with a little milk.

As Aziza was busy thinking, her eye fell on that strange face which she had carved out, during one of the many tedious nights in her solitary cell, on a black wall which had not seen a coat of paint for many years, using rusty nails which she had picked up one day in the prison courtyard. She never knew why she had drawn this face with its unfamiliar features, which did not resemble anyone she had known before, but looking at it at this particular time, she recalled an incident which had taken place years ago and had remained buried in her memory. This process of calling up old memories was not unusual either for her or, almost certainly, for all those other weak and feeble inmates locked behind the high walls and cut off from the accumulation of new memories in the outside world. In this respect it was as if they were dying, cut off from hope and unable to hold on to life, through regenerating the images in their minds.

Aziza remembered an incident in her childhood when her beloved stepfather took her on a trip from Alexandria to Cairo during which they wandered round all the sights of the city. They went to the ancient part of Cairo where the conqueror Amr landed, and they went to the Hanging Church and the Synagogue which were a lasting proof of the fortress's surrender and the conquest of the city which has long been used to paying taxes to its conquerors. They visited the verdant area of Helwan, its Japanese garden with the four statues, and made a tour of all the city's gardens, now lost amongst the crowds and general neglect for everything which is green, natural and beautiful. They went to the Andalusian garden with ponds full of ornamental fish and dark, secret caves where her lover had surprised her with sweet kisses she would never forget. They visited the Azbekiyya garden and the zoo where she saw a zebra for the first time. She saw amazing peacocks and wanted one of her own, a wish that came only too true when time was to prove that for her stepfather she was nothing but a peacock herself.

Aziza also remembered her visit to the pyramids and the sphinx and especially her visit to the Pharaonic Museum which had left an indelible mark. As she sat in her cell she tried to call up scenes from her past life and unravel the pattern of threads woven in the recesses of her memory.

Her head was full of all the trips she made with her lover when they walked hand in hand like any couple who have been openly in love for a long time. Aziza conjured up the statue of a huge woman, with an ample, fertile body and the head of a cow whose face was kind and gentle. She was hugging a little baby and the image rose up strongly from the recesses of Aziza's memory, taking shape before her eyes just as she saw it all that time ago. She remembered questioning her lover at the time about the statue, and the reply he gave her as he hugged her to him: "It's an ancient goddess, Hathur, dedicated to beauty and fertility, who was worshipped for many years. She is showing compassion for the little holy god she is carrying, Hurus."

Aziza gazed at what she had drawn on the wall which had brought to her the memory of the ancient statue and told her story to Umm El-Khayr as if she were in front of her in the cell. She told her how she remembered standing at that moment trying to make sense of the confusion she felt as she touched her breasts with her hand, searching inside her for the meaning of the word "fertility" which she had heard for the first time in her life from the lips of her lover.

Aziza had never been able to imagine that she could ever be like that kindly human cow which embraced children with its care and compassion. She always believed that she had been created for something else, which proved to be the case. It was as if she had mapped out her destiny on that distant day when she decided that she would not be like that statue in the shape of a cow. Yet now she discovered that the image she had drawn on the wall resembled that statue buried in her memory. Furthermore she had conjured up Umm El-Khayr to sit before her that night replete with all the mothering instincts she possessed which engulfed everyone around her, including Aziza. Umm El-Khayr treated all the women she came into contact with in the prison as her daughters, including those amongst them who were older than she was; her maternal instinct even extended to the pampered prison cat. Aziza had never known the meaning of this feeling since she had never experienced it first hand. From that day in her distant childhood she had decided that she had been created for passion rather than fertility – a passion she was to dedicate herself to and which would lead to murder and madness.

Until Aziza encountered Umm El-Khayr's overflowing maternal love she had been completely unaware of such qualities, having never experienced this kind of love, even from her mother, who was more like an older sister to her. Her feelings towards her mother were not unlike those of a young girl who looks up to her older, more experienced friend. It was a unique relationship blessed with harmony and linked by a fine thread which placed them on an equal footing – a thread personified in the stepfather, the one man they both loved without any sign of strife or conflict, who gave equally to each of them. His generosity included presents, magnificent clothes, and evening expeditions to the most splendid shops in Alexandria, at a time when it was still a city known as "the heart of the world", which attracted people from all over and where the prosperous élite of the country lived. Last but not least the man they shared never stinted either of them with his body. As a result Aziza had never thought of this woman as a mother since they took and gave equally. Even though Aziza enjoyed the sexual and other favours granted by her stepfather, this did not inhibit her mother's enjoyments of the same. Nor did the mother regard her daughter as the source of joy and solace in her life. Deprived, though she was, of the blessing of sight she did not seek to compensate for this by using her daughter's eyes.

However this person sitting in front of her, Umm El-Khayr, was the true mother goddess, at this moment visible only to Aziza through her imagination which was now weary and impaired through years of painful seclusion. She was maternal love personified, who gave unconditionally, nurturing everyone through her love, particularly her beloved sons. Through the rings of smoke rising in front of her, the image of Umm El-Khayr took on the form of that huge old statue of the woman cow-goddess whose name Aziza had for the moment completely forgotten despite her repeated attempts to extract it from the torn web of her memories, full of sadness and scattered moments of joy which shone like a light through mellowed wine. The difference between the real statue and the woman of flesh and blood was in that milk which gushed out from her nipples and which would soon cover her until it flowed profusely across the floor between her feet, forming a small stream which Aziza saw stretching beyond the door of the cell, forging a path along the long tiled corridor, leading to the other cells. Aziza bent down to the floor to lap it up. It intoxicated her more than any wine she had drunk in the past, and she craved it as never before. When her tongue licked the old tiled floor of the cell and she felt the rough cracks against her tongue, hot tears began to fall and she did not lift her head until she had released all the pent-up pain and suffering which had accumulated inside her.

Since that unforgettable evening full of sadness and after she had become accustomed to the long nights in prison, Aziza was convinced that Umm El-Khayr was none other than one of those ancient revered goddesses who had fallen from heaven into the women's prison in order to save the lost souls tormented by loneliness, banishment and exile and to comfort them with her overflowing compassion. This cherished view was reinforced by the relationship, which Aziza considered supernatural, between the prison cat, which after all was a dumb animal, and Umm El-Khayr. She decided that it could only exist because Umm El-Khayr was a goddess. The cat slept most days with her nose resting next to Umm El-Khayr's face without being rebuffed; Aziza often heard her chatting to the cat and delivering words of comfort when the male cats ate her young ones in their nightly raids on the wards while she was out searching for something to eat to replenish the milk in her teats for her young. Most of the prisoners showed tenderness towards this cat, perhaps because they were deprived of the chance to express their feelings towards their loved ones and they enjoyed the affection the cat showed in return when it brushed against their legs and miaowed softly, especially when they threw her a few of their meagre left-overs or stroked her back gently. But Aziza noticed that the cat singled out Umm El-Khayr for special affection, that secret kind which Aziza immediately recognized, and which could only be granted to goddesses. This apricot-coloured cat, with her dark eyes and her tail which had lost a few inches after a violent fight that took place one night with a vicious old cat and lasted until dawn, liked to spend every night in Umm El-Khayr's bed under her feet. She watched over Umm El-Khayr and kept guard over her as she slept, like a guardian angel. One night she caught a naïve, unsuspecting mouse which had slipped into the cardboard box which Umm El-Khayr used to store her possessions; on another occasion she pulled out a huge poisonous spider from one of her plastic shoes, a recent invention to guard against going bare foot as people have done for seven thousand years, just as Umm El-Khayr was about to slip her foot, with its cracked sole worn from treading the rough soil, into the shoe.

The secret relationship between the cat and Umm El-Khayr was only one of the extraordinary, superhuman aspects that Aziza discovered about this peasant-goddess. She also possessed amazing patience, which might only be compared to the endurance of a very old cactus tree, and which was particularly noticeable in her dealings with that wretched young Saïdi woman, Aida. Everyone in prison recognized that

Aida suffered from a strange neurosis which had made her suddenly lose her memory and which sometimes caused her mind to wander for several hours or even days. Her forgetfulness reached the point where she did not even remember her name and was unable to recognize those around her. Nor could she cope with everyday things, which brought her many problems and made her an object of ridicule for some of the prisoners who found her condition a fertile source of jokes and laughter, particularly when she did eccentric things. One time she slept with a small plastic bowl, turned upside down, under her head instead of a pillow; on another occasion she made tea for Mahrousa, the warden, when she came to sit with her on her bed in the ward, but instead of adding sugar she put two spoonfuls of black pepper in it. Were it not for Mahrousa's good nature and her sympathy for Aida's condition, she would have slapped her hard on her face, like any other warder who would have considered such behaviour from a prisoner as insolent.

Aziza understood the full extent of Umm El-Khayr's patience and the untiring compassion she showed towards the prisoners on the day she asked Umm El-Khayr about Aida's story. Umm El-Khayr told her that Aida was a poor, miserable young girl who had experienced unimaginable traumas and horrors which had left her an orphan although she still had close relations. After she lost everything she lived without hope and perhaps the proverb that described her situation best was the saying: "When the flood comes stand on your children's shoulders." When the origin of this proverb and how it applied to Aida the Saïdi was made clear to Aziza, her mind turned to the heavenly voyage and she made a secret decision to include Aida. Umm El-Khayr sighed and asked Aziza to bless the Prophet – peace and blessings be upon Him – and when this had been done and repeated a second time at Umm El-Khayr's request, the wise peasant began to tell the story. She said: "Once upon a time in a certain field, a rabbit lived with his sons in a burrow under a tall sycamore tree at the edge of the field. One day the rabbit asked one of his children to go out and keep watch on the path and the field and, once he was sure that the coast was clear and that there were no humans around, he should come back quickly to inform his father so that he could go with him and his brothers to the field to feed and play with them happily without fear.

When the little rabbit went out and looked around the field he saw no living creature apart from an old fox roaming around looking for prey. When the little rabbit saw him, he thought it would be better to ask him if he had seen anyone in the field or anywhere near so that he could reassure his father when he went back. So the rabbit said hello to the fox and told him why he was there and asked if there were any humans around. The fox had decided to kill him as soon as he set eyes on him because he was extremely hungry and was longing to gobble him up but he held back because he thought that the rabbit must have a burrow close to the field where he lived with his brothers. It would be wiser to find out where it was so that he could slink up to it every night and seize one of the rabbits for his dinner, thereby saving himself the effort of searching for prey. He resolved to follow a crafty plan in his dealings with the little rabbit, telling him that although he hadn't seen anyone since dawn, he feared that on his way back to his father he might meet a human who would harm him, perhaps even kill him, and that this would cause his father terrible worry and grief. Thus he offered to accompany the rabbit to his burrow to make sure that he got back safely.

So the fox set off with the little rabbit, who was extremely happy with this arrangement. On the way, the fox chatted with him and told him the story of the gullible black duck who lived in a barn with lots of geese, cocks and hens. She noticed how white the geese were and how red the hens were and she noticed the magnificent colours of the ornamental cocks, and this made her feel discontented because she was pitch-black and life had denied her the luck of being colourful like the others. One day she saw a dog which was showing considerable interest in the animals as they came out of the barn into the courtyard of the house; he was also guarding the geese as they came to have a swim. He asked the duck why she was troubled and annoyed and when she told him he advised her to slip into the storehouse and dip herself secretly into the flour basket; once she was covered with flour she would emerge pure white like milk. These words pacified the duck who went back to the barn full of joy.

The next day, the duck went to the storehouse and buried herself in the flour basket. She exhausted herself through the huge effort she made to make sure that her head and all her feathers were smothered with fine particles of flour. When she returned to the barn, the owner of the house opened the door for the geese to go to the river nearby and the duck rushed to catch up with the geese. She wanted to swim with them and to enjoy washing herself in the cold water so that she could be clean and beautiful like them. When she reached the river and saw the white geese swimming she looked at herself with satisfaction; with her true blackness concealed by the fine white grains she felt beautiful like the geese. But when she got into the water, the white flour sticking to her began to dissolve revealing the original blackness of her feathers. Once the duck realized what had happened she got out of the river and went back to the barn, mortified. The furious owner of the house was waiting for her with a knife in her hand since she had decided to slaughter the duck for dinner after discovering that she had gone into the flour basket and ruined all the flour the owner had stored to use for baking.

When the rabbit and fox reached the burrow beneath the tree, the rabbit said goodbye to him and entered the burrow while the fox remained hidden outside by a tree, watching the burrow for any activity. The little rabbit, meanwhile, was telling his father what had happened with the fox and when his father heard the story and understood its significance, his heart sank because he knew that danger was near and that disaster was about to befall them; the fox would undoubtedly attack the burrow from every side and devour them. He began to think frantically and then he looked at his son sadly and told him: "Go out of the burrow again and you will find the fox waiting for you. Tell him as soon as you see him that you didn't find your father and brothers in the burrow and that they have probably gone to another burrow somewhere far away from the field. Then ask him to go with you there, just as he came here with you, and when you are well on your way, leave him and come back quickly and we will be waiting for you."

As the little rabbit went out of the burrow his father was in no doubt that he was doomed. He saw the fox racing towards the far off burrow which they would never find and knew that when the fox discovered the trick he would be furious and gobble up the little rabbit. So as soon as the fox and the rabbit had disappeared from view, the old rabbit ran off with all his children and escaped with them from the burrow and field to a far away place out of range of the fox. Knowing that he had sacrificed the little rabbit he said to himself: "If the flood comes, stand on your child's shoulders."

At the end of this story, Umm El-Khayr said to Aziza: "What happened to the little rabbit, is what happened to the poor Saïdi girl, Aida. Consider the wisdom of God because what happens in the world of animals can also happen in the world of humans." Then she went on to tell Aziza what, exactly, had happened to Aida. She sat with her back against the wall of the adjacent ward, basking in the sun and amusing herself by playing ball with little pieces of brick to distract herself from the boredom which inevitably arose from being shut up and enclosed. Mishmisha, the cat, stretched out peacefully next to her on top of the most recent line in winter fashion illustrated on the woman's page of the weekly edition of Al-Ahram, following the little ball as it was juggled in the air. Then Umm El-Khayr told how she heard a strange sound which resembled the pained wailing of an Armant dog in labour. She knew that there were no dogs in the prison because, unlike cats, they were unable to leap far enough to get over the high walls or get through the main door which was within the earshot and scrutiny of the guards. Nevertheless she had got up from her seat on the floor thinking that perhaps there really was a dog somewhere in the prison which had given birth. Her amazement grew after she had gone only a few steps and found Aida, sitting in front of a basin staring vacantly and making the noise of a bitch wailing. She was gnawing a piece of dark prison soap with a degree of violence that expressed the pain felt by a bitch expelling a litter of seven puppies from her womb.

Umm El-Khayr described how she ran quickly to Aida to remove the soap from her mouth before she swallowed it. She pressed her thin cheeks with her strong hands, the hands which had so often gripped a hoe to break up the soil and till it, until she was able to force Aida to spit out all the soap in her mouth. When she was sure that all that remained in Aida's mouth were those few teeth separated by gaps and the small, dry tongue which caused her to stammer, Umm El-Khayr released her from her grip gently telling her to scream with all her might to expel all the sadness and pain suppressed within her. Before she fainted, Aida let out a cry which built up to a crescendo of pain and sorrow and which, had anyone been around to take any notice of her at the time, which of course they weren't, might have made them think she was something to do with the opera.

The same evening she was moved to sleep temporarily in the ward for the disabled, in an area specially designated as the prison hospital. Aida, who remained in shock, remembered nothing of the day's events and had lost her appetite, but told her story to Umm El-Khayr who had remained constantly by her side, handing her some sweetened lemon to drink to refresh her and rubbing the palms of her hands and the soles of her feet to make the blood circulate after they had turned blue and cold as ice. Aida only spoke after Umm El-Khayr had convinced her that the suppression of her pain would lead to insanity. Umm El-Khayr urged her to trust and lean on her as a mother, whose support for her child outweighs any other consideration. When Aida heard these words they touched the secret wound in her heart and the floodgates opened, rivalling any performance given by the Egyptian actress, Amina Razaq, who was the queen of tears. Aida threw herself into Umm El-Khayr's arms, just as a daughter would do with her real mother, and unburdened herself. In a theatrical scene that verged on tragedy she shouted that she had never had a mother, a revelation which made Umm El-Khayr cry out in torment and draw Aida closely to her.

The prisoners knew that Aida had been sent to prison having been sentenced to life with hard labour for murdering her husband but the details and reasons for this were only known after Umm El-Khayr pieced together the whole story. Once this had occurred, and without the slightest embarrassment or fear, Aida started to tell her own story to any prisoner so that it should not remain locked inside her, eating away at her. The ceaseless torments which she had suffered had begun to imprint themselves on her features and not even her dark eyes and striking bushy eyebrows were enough to detract from her defeated look. Her long jet-black Ayrian hair dangled over her pallid face, which was tinged with blue and prematurely wrinkled for a woman not yet thirty. The pain within her drove her to the point of breakdown and to the brink of madness.

Aida was twenty-three years old when her family decided to marry her off to her cousin, who was at least twenty years older than her. This happened following a visit from her uncle and his wife, who often boasted that she was descended from the Prophet. After they had taken tea with her mother and father the two men read the opening verse of the Qur'an to celebrate the first stage of the engagement and her mother went round the house trilling triumphantly so that all the neighbours would be aware of the happy event. After that she called Aida and kissed her in front of everyone in the reception room, with the set of Assiuti chairs and the nine large framed photographs of her father, her brothers and some of the other relations who had died many years ago. After everyone had congratulated her, her father said: "Congratulations, Aida, your uncle has betrothed you to his son, Mansi", and her mother and future mother-in-law made enormous efforts to see who could trill longest and loudest.

Aida neither hated nor loved Mansi because she simply didn't know him. When she was small and still allowed to play with boys, he was a young man who came to visit them on rare occasions as a messenger from his father to his uncle on family business. If she went with her mother and brother to their house he rarely sat with them because her own brother was much younger than him. In the years immediately before her engagement she had not seen him as he was away for long periods working as a teacher in another town far from their village.

Before the wedding, she had obtained a diploma in commerce. Immediately after she obtained her diploma, her uncle hurried to put in hand the preparations for the wedding. Her mother behaved like a hen who had just layed an egg, bursting with pride because the bridegroom, as the only male amongst three children, would inherit the lion's share of his father's estate. In addition, by giving private lessons to students he was earning enough to enable him to contribute towards the cost of furnishing the future marital home, something which a bridegroom is not normally obliged to do. As well as the usual carpets, chandeliers and kitchen furniture, the bridegroom also undertook to install a fan on the ceiling in one of the rooms. Moreover, at considerable cost he had the walls hung with embossed wallpaper which, even though it clashed with what her mother had chosen for the entrance hall, was generally considered by the members of the family to be both extremely tasteful and a work of art. He then bought all the necessary electrical appliances for the house from the proceeds of his private lessons, received monthly from the families of his students. In turn, these students received doses of learning privately to supplement the normal school lessons, which were often unsatisfactory.

The bridegroom splashed out on everything which in his view was needed to have a comfortable life, from a gas igniter to an electric shaver, and he was the first person in the village to buy a video. On this famous day he celebrated his new purchase by showing the film "Ismail Yasin in the Army" to his mother, father and sisters as well as a number of relations and neighbours who filled his father's big old house and during which they consumed a large packet of Lipton tea and a whole kilo of sugar.

Before the wedding, Aida realized that her husband had been extremely spoilt by his mother and father but she never imagined that he had a cruel harsh nature which emerged as soon as they were married and started an intimate relationship. It was then that she realized why her brother had been so unenthusiastic about the marriage and had even tried to dissuade her father from going through with it. He had suggested that the cousin's proposal to his sister had been accepted in a hurry and that she could make a much better match. But the father took his son's advice both as a slur on his honour and an insult to his brother and nephew, swearing three times to divorce his mother and to banish him from the house for ever should he ever broach the subject again.

Aida's special relationship with her only brother was unusual amongst brothers and sisters in their native area of the distant Saïd. Her brother had a gentle nature and his manner towards her did not exhibit that sense of inequality which is such a feature in relations between a boy and a girl, despite the fact that they were brought up in a male-dominated environment in which the girl is traditionally denied any real rights, is little esteemed and considered fit only for bearing children. Maybe this was because they were so close in age – he was only ten months younger than her – and because there had never been the prospect of further children, his mother having had a hysterectomy after his birth. Their father had always threatened to marry again in order to sire more children and their mother's constant references to this made them anxious from the time they were little. When Aida moved to her new home on the wedding night, her feelings of sadness and loss were not due to leaving her parents nor because she was moving away from the place in which she had grown up, but were, rather, due to her separation from her only brother, who was her soulmate and had been her constant companion since the time they were little children. Accordingly the feelings of love and longing which Aida felt for her only brother increased sharply and may well have played a part in the growing hatred and revulsion she felt towards her husband. From the start of their marriage she had felt at odds with him. When her family had left them alone and she sat next to him for dinner, she was astonished by his excessive greed. He consumed a whole duck, a pair of stuffed pigeons with green wheat, cooked in the local style that her mother had prepared for them, leaving her only the leftovers. As for his attempts at seduction and love-making, they made her feel as if she was one of those women dancers at the saints' festivals. She had often heard about their behaviour and what men do with them, men who pay them for a quick moment of pleasure. She hated him at that time and she hated the way he fondled her. She felt that he defiled her the way a pure prayer mat is defiled by the feet of a filthy pig.

Two months into the marriage and before she could become pregnant any children, disagreements became part of their everyday life. Often, for a variety of reasons, mostly trivial, he would lash out and hit her. One such occasion was when Aida put the jam jar in the fridge, even though he had repeatedly told her that he didn't like his jam when it was chilled, and another time she went to sleep with unsweetened gum in her mouth which infuriated him because her saliva tasted bitter when he kissed her. The truth was that Aida did not do these things deliberately to annoy him or consciously to challenge him but because she suffered from simple forgetfulness – a condition which was to become so acute in prison that she beame lost to the world.

Aida often complained about her husband to her mother because she was the woman closest to her. She showed her the bruises on her body to demonstrate the violence which her husband inflicted on her, but her mother always refused to intervene, urging her to remain silent lest her father get to hear about it. She blamed her daughter for not putting herself out for him and for not allowing for the fact that her husband was a spoilt, only son. If she were clever she would have turned him into the ring of Solomon on her hand, but because she was stubborn as a donkey she did not appreciate her God-given fortune and the fact that she was married to someone from a good family with excellent inheritance prospects and a good job. She went on to say that she was the envy of all the girls in the village and that it was arrogant and ungrateful of her to behave like this considering she was dark and had very little in the way of breasts or bottom. If it weren't for the fine black hair she had inherited and her widely-set eyes, no man would ever have given her a second look and if her husband had not been the well-bred man that he was and hadn't been so keen to marry within the family, his power and influence could have enabled him to find a fair-skinned girl of his choice who was more beautiful and sweet-natured than her.

Aida was never convinced by her mother's words, always delivered in the customary harsh manner which she had resented since childhood. Whenever her aunt came to visit them she had always been amazed at her mother's failure to defend her when her aunt made fun of her dark skin and her slight body. She would comment, in a mocking tone, that she couldn't believe such a daughter could come from her sister's womb and that she must have stumbled across her amongst the rubble in a coal merchant's shop. Poor Aida saw that her mother became even more determined to distance herself from her problems and to make sure that her brother, her only friend, took the same line in the matter. She warned her against allowing her brother to intercede on her behalf with her husband, pointing out the danger of this leading to a disagreement between them which might rupture relations between them. This made Aida determined to hide all her marital problems from her brother and to put on a show of enthusiasm for a married life which was, in reality, unbearable.

After a year of marriage when Aida was still not pregnant and showed no signs of producing the child her husband desired, her difficulties with her husband reached a climax. The problem, so far as her husband was concerned, was that he could not marry another woman quickly because of the huge outlay he had made in furnishing the matrimonial home and in investing in his cherished dream and wish of living a quiet and comfortable life. He began to insinuate that his wife must be sterile, an allegation which was completely unfounded: in fact two doctors who had each opened private clinics a few years after graduating, told her that she was perfectly capable of having children. She also went with her sister to a reputable woman doctor who told her that her ovulation might be a little weak, advising her to have some tests, while at the same time suggesting that her husband should also be examined. But when she returned home and repeated what the doctor had told her, he waited until her sister had left then slapped her very hard on the face, accusing her of insolence and disrespect which degraded his manliness. He stressed that if he had decided long ago to marry another woman, who was a real woman, capable of getting pregnant and giving birth, she would have have produced a dozen children for him by now. That night, as he tried to demonstrate his virility several times in spite of the extreme revulsion she felt for him, her wish that he would die first became a concrete desire as she willed a plague or some awful disease to strike him down and lift him from the spot where he sat.

Aida was overjoyed when her mother informed her two years later that her husband had disclosed his desire to marry another woman. She saw this new development as a happy solution to her problems which would put an end to the worries she never thought she would be rid of so easily. Her mother was surprised at her reaction and accused her of being stupid and cold-hearted; any other woman in her place would be crying and bemoaning her fate and shattered hopes. When she returned home that day after visiting her mother and learning of her husband's intentions she felt lighthearted and joyous. This became obvious by the cheerful way she received her husband when he returned late that night from his teaching; she had laid out his dinner and offered to prepare a hot bath to soothe him after his exertion. This sense of euphoria lasted for several days while she was still hopeful that he would broach the subject of his intended marriage. At this point she would tell him: "Be happy with God's blessing" and that she was in complete agreement on condition that he divorce her and allow her to return to her father's home to live in peace and quiet. But one night he came home earlier than usual and asked her to make a cup of tea for him. He then began to speak gently to her which was quite out of character and admired her hairdo which was no different from usual. He told her that after thinking the matter over and praying for guidance he had come to the conclusion that he was about to take a step he might regret for the rest of his life. He had wanted to marry someone else but had recovered his senses and abandoned this evil thought, telling her: "Aida, you are my kith and kin and it is my duty to protect you." He began to speak in glowing terms about the qualities of her character which were unrivalled and praised her ability to endure the ups and downs of life with him. Then he suggested she should go to a famous doctor in Cairo who specializes in sterility, offering to foot the bill for any treatment prescribed because he was no longer convinced by these local doctors of limited experience nor by all the traditional remedies which she followed on the advice of her mother and elder sister. As he noisily gulped down the last mouthful of tea he dropped the bombshell: if, God willing, she were to become pregnant he would slaughter a buffalo calf before the shrine in Cairo of Sayyida Umm El-Ghulam, the patron saint of children and those that loved them and he would distribute the meat to the poor and the vagrants of the quarter.

Her husband's change of mind about marrying again ruined his chance of fulfilling his ambition to father a child, while Aida lost any chance of retrieving peace of mind. The old violence which had existed between them was re-kindled after the temporary remission which had only been sustained by her hope of the new marriage taking place. Aida's feelings of desperation returned and her husband reverted to abusing her and invented new sadistic ways of beating her. He sometimes hit her with his leather belt and sometimes with a reed cane which he drew quickly out of his briefcase to inflict on some part of her body; this was the cane which he used on the adolescent boys at the secondary school where he taught. One day he discovered that she had washed twenty pounds and his membership card for the Workers' Union which he had left in one of his trouser pockets, having forgotten to check them before washing. When he upbraided her for this she replied in all honesty and without fear or remorse that she had simply forgotten to inspect the pockets at which point he swore at her and hit her until he drew blood. But this instance of violence differed from all the previous times since the doorbell suddenly rang in the middle of it all. Aida took advantage of the lull in violence to hide in the bathroom, the blood streaming from her nose and face, while her husband went to answer the door. It was none other than Aida's brother bringing two bags of bananas and oranges. He was accompanied by her mother carrying a dish of *baklava* carefully wrapped in coloured paper displaying the name of the sweet shop they came from – a simple gift which she offered with profuse greetings to the young married couple.

As soon as her brother came through the door, he noticed drops of blood on the floor and asked after his sister who came out to seek protection from the visitors. When he saw her unkempt hair, her tearful eyes and bloody nose with her right eye bruised and her swollen lips, he could not contain his anger and rushed at her husband and began to hit him. Her husband, who was still beside himself with fury, rushed to the kitchen and returned carrying the large knife which Aida had so often used to slaughter the chickens. By this time her brother had become so enraged that he was like a bull about to charge and, although surprised when Aida's husband descended on him with the knife and tried to plunge into his chest, he managed to wrest it from him and stabbed him repeatedly until he fell lifeless like the buffalo calf which the husband had intended to sacrifice to Umm El-Ghulam.

Aida tried to scream but although she had opened her mouth wide she could only produce a strained moaning sound. She rushed to try and remove the knife which had been sunk into her husband's side, who was on the point of death. But her mother, who had entered the apartment and locked the door behind her, intervened quickly between them to prevent her approaching him. It was as if she had planned the whole business in advance. However, the truth was that as a Saïdi woman from an isolated village she was well versed, from first-hand knowledge, in the rules of the vendetta. She calmly instructed her daughter to back off, confident of her wisdom in these matters, saying: "Move away . . . it's better if he dies."

Her son, with his slight body which resembled his sister's, collapsed into the nearest available chair with sweat pouring from his deathly pale face. His cunning mother shook him violently, telling him to wipe the sweat away and pull himself together; this was not the time to collapse. She turned matters over in her mind, calculating everything as if her head contained some Japanese precision instrument. Then she turned to her daughter, whose mouth still hung open with the violent shock and terror she had suffered, saying in a voice of steel: "Listen to me. The disaster has happened. Thank God he is dead because if he had lived the affair would have become a drama without end. So listen, daughter, to every word that I say to you and carry out my instructions from beginnning to end so that the police don't discover the truth and one disaster doesn't lead to another."

The mother's plan was simple and did not require great skill to execute but she was very efficient all the same. After she had wiped the traces left by her son's hand on the handle of the knife, she ordered Aida to slip her right hand through her hair which was greased with castor oil and to take hold of the knife as if it were she who had carried out the killing. This followed after she had convinced Aida that her brother was not to blame for what happened and that the fault was hers because she had ignored her advice and done nothing to smooth matters over by trying to reach some understanding with her husband. She had begged her to take the rough with the smooth especially as she was barren; he was a good, patient man who accepted his lot which had deprived him of having a son to carry on his name and restore his reputation for virility. Thus it was up to her to solve the problem and save her brother from tragedy; she should take responsibility and confess to the killing, whereupon her confession before the police and the prosecution would settle the matter. Because of the code of the vendetta, if it ever became known that her brother was the murderer this would release a torrent of blood which might flow without end in their family and that of her uncle. No one in their community paid any regard to government procedures and court sentences, and her husband's father would undoutedly seek to avenge his son by killing her brother. The whole affair would reach a point where the sons of one family would sort it out with those of the other and all the men would be annihilated because of her. No one would take revenge on her and the court would only sentence her to a few years in prison because she would say that she never planned her husband's murder but had killed him in self-defence.

The mother did not tell her daughter the rest of the plan which Aida discovered later, and had never stopped thinking about, even at the very moment she bit into the black prison soap. The crime shook the village community who never dreamt that an incident of this kind could occur in such a respectable home. After the police inspected the scene of the crime they took Aida away in a car to the department dealing with the investigation. Her mother promised to instruct the best lawyer in Cairo to defend her and protect her interests until the conclusion of the trial, adding that she would never abandon her during her imprisonment. But the reality, which Aida never anticipated, was something completely different. Despite the long time which had passed she never believed that her mother and father could have abandoned her as soon as she had been sentenced to life imprisonment nor that they had washed their hands of her forever as a murderer who respected neither God nor the ties of kinship. Even worse, that they both considered her dead without granting her the ceremony of mourning. To the delight of the family of the murdered son, the gentle young brother was coerced by his parents into marrying the victim's sister, despite the fact that she was a widow nine years older than him and was crippled by polio. Aida tried to contact them in various ways and sent them dozens of letters; she even sent news via someone from their village whom she met in prison and was released after serving half of her sentence on good behaviour. But days and months followed without her receiving a single word from these people with their hearts of stone. This silence completely destroyed her and made her curse the moment she submitted against her better judgement to her mother's diabolical plan and agreed to confess to the crime. She had hesitated at the time out of fear but her mother's scornful looks which pierced her, heart and soul, terrified her into submisssion. She also feared for her beloved brother who only killed her husband out of compassion for her and out of concern for her loss of dignity.

After Aida had lost all hope of retrieving any thread which tied her to her family and her old world, she fell prey to grief and began to crave death. She longed to see her beloved brother to whom she had often sent letters seeking his compassion and begging him to reply. What hurt her most was that his loving tender heart which was always compassionate towards her could have bowed to the influence of his parents in agreeing to abandon her. How could he be so heartless as to forget her and leave her to this terrible place without sending a word? She hoped for nothing more in life but to see him face to face once more and to look into his beautiful eyes and chide him for his harshness towards her since she had only accepted the role of murderess for his sake and for the sake of protecting him from further harm.

However, one day – the very day she ate the soap – she met a smelter by chance in the prison kitchen whom she immediately recognized because he lived in the same street as her in the village where she was married. She knew he had also been sentenced to life imprisonment, for stealing telephone cables, and was an inmate of the adjoining men's prison. Passionately, she began to beg him for news of her family and he told her that both her mother and father were well and so were her uncle and his wife but when she asked him about her brother, who concerned her more than all the others, he hesitated a little then told her that he was dead. His wife had tried to rouse him from his sleep one morning and was surprised to get no response. When she tried again she discovered that he was dead and the doctor diagnosed a sudden heart attack which had killed him in his sleep. However, the whole village said that his wife had poisoned him with a rare poison which leaves no trace in the body nor in any of its organs. On hearing this Aida left him, dragging her feet to the prison courtyard and stood with her mouth wide open just as she did when her brother killed her husband. She soon went back to her ward and gathered together the few clothes that she owned together with her white sheets and went to wash them, even though they weren't dirty. She set about scrubbing them energetically, as the best way she knew of getting rid of her frustration and of unburdening the suppressed feelings that she had harboured over the period when life had been so cruel to her. But despite washing the clothes until they were thoroughly clean and scrubbing them over and over again, the washing neither alleviated her troubles nor satisfied her, and in no way assuaged the pain which burned inside her. It was for this reason that she had been unable to control herself and had begun to howl like a bitch in labour. The pain caused her to cry out, tearing her soul to shreds, and even though she had never experienced labour pains in her life, she started stomach contractions as if she were really giving birth. At this point she began to eat the soap because it seemed preferable to the earth she was sitting on, she would have swallowed it had it not been for Umm El-Khayr, who came and prised open her jaws. From that moment she was aware of nothing more until she opened her eyes again to find herself on a bed in the prison hospital.

All the while Aziza listened to Aida's story she was gazing at the ground, occasionally interposing a few words to reassure Umm El-Khayr that she was still listening and following. As she listened to the tale, she mulled over the extent of pain and sadness which this young woman had suffered because her family had shut her out of their hearts. What astonished her the most was the amazing cruelty of the mother and her rejection and desertion of her daughter in such difficult circumstances. She was shocked by the rigid traditions of the Saïd and the insistence on taking blood revenge, when neither life nor retribution really worked like that. There is a law unknown to conventional justice whereby revenge can surface in a thousand different ways. It is possible for the victim to take revenge on the wrongdoer simply by invading his being with remorse and thereby tormenting his conscience and soul.

Then time takes its own revenge on everything in life by constantly transforming what appears to be unchangeable, just as the maternal love of Aida's mother was transformed into extreme cruelty.

Umm El-Khayr related Aida's story factually and without any embellishment. When she had finished she asked for God's protection from the Devil and raised her hands in supplication asking for health and protection for her ten children and that He should bless them with good people around them who would take care of them in their daily life. Meanwhile, after the most intense and prolonged thought, Aziza had decided to include Aida in the golden chariot. However she decided not to tell Umm El-Khayr immediately, preferring to keep her in suspense for a little. So she asked her to apply her gentle and skilled hands in making a pudding of rice flour, dried milk, sugar and corn-starch. When this was prepared she stood up and handed her a little sugar on a dish for them to share with the pudding, whispering to her, "Tell Aida, but keep it to yourselves, that, God willing, she will be coming with us." Umm El-Khayr didn't give what Aziza said a second thought, refusing to take anything she said seriously because she believed Aziza was half-witted.

4

An Escape to Better Things in the Golden Chariot

The old white tiled floor in Aziza the Alexandrian's ward looked sparkling clean even though it was faded through the wear and tear of time; Jamalat had just finished scrubbing it with a piece of sackcloth and water, mixed with a little liquid chlorine in the absence of any other disinfectants like carbolic acid which Aziza preferred because it gave a good shine and cleaned well. Unfortunately carbolic acid was not allowed because it came in dark bottles, instead of transparent plastic containers which couldn't harm anyone in the violent incidents which broke out between the prisoners from time to time.

Aziza looked with pleasure at the damp, clean tiled floor, so cool at this hot time of the year, and her eye followed the thin, curved wainscot along the edge. She had just voluntarily given up her small iron bed to one of the political prisoners she came across from time to time. She could see no obvious reason why such people should be dumped there or why the Government should be on collision course with them. This political prisoner was extremely friendly to Aziza and one day she greeted her as she passed her in the corridor where Aziza was standing with Azima the giant. After the political prisoner had given her a broad, friendly smile Aziza felt encouraged to approach her to discover her story. She guessed she might be a communist or belong to the Muslim Brotherhood because they were the only kind of political prisoners Aziza had met during her long stay in prison.

She soon came to the conclusion that she must be a communist because she was not veiled and seemed rather lively and straightforward. The girl spoke to her in the same way that all the other communists Aziza had met in prison before had done; she never understood anything they said to her, nor the purpose of the mental and physical anguish that women like this girl brought upon themselves. Aziza noticed that almost all of them were educated and respectable. They had good jobs and lived in more pleasant circumstances than most; she observed the lavish visits they had every other day and the cigarettes which arrived for most of them in cartons of two hundred. Now she felt annoyed with herself because she no longer understood things as she had before; she was distracted and her mind was in turmoil.

Aziza sighed, she found it rather a strain to listen to the girl's story which had nothing new in it as far as she was concerned. She had heard the same story from many others before and had concluded that such stories were good for nothing – useless – because, if the truth be told, these politically-minded people lived in another world and knew absolutely nothing about the poor they were always talking about. She looked over into the girl's cell and noticed there was no bed in it – only a straw mattress lying on the floor. The political prisoner then asked her about her story and Aziza told her an abridged version; the girl gave her another smile and wished her well, presenting her with a whole packet of Marlboro cigarettes. Aziza was overwhelmed by her generosity and began to think of how she could reciprocate; after returning to her cell she decided to give her her iron bed since Aziza saw little difference between sleeping on a bed raised from the ground or on her mattress directly on the tiled floor, particularly as the summer heat was intense at that time. Aziza decided that she could accompany her on the golden chariot with winged horses at the moment of lift-off to heaven. Aziza actually carried out her first idea and asked Jamalat and Azima, the mourner, to carry the bed and place it in the political prisoner's ward. However, her second idea was aborted by the Government's decision to release the girl only a month after her imprisonment. Aziza bitterly regretted not having informed her about the heavenly ascent before she had received the order for her release. There was no doubt in her mind that the girl would have been so taken with the idea that she would not have left prison but would have joined the passengers on the chariot ascending to the beautiful celestial world, the like of which could never be found on earth.

However, after thinking about it a little, Aziza thanked God that the girl had left prison, for if she really had joined the chariot she would almost certainly have talked incessantly about politics and incited all the passengers to demonstrate against their contemptible conditions in prison. This would have enraged the government and, even if the chariot had taken off into the clouds, it could have aborted the ascent by sending one of its many planes to arrest the girl.

Aziza inspected her large room carefully, and after she was satisfied that her few possessions, just old clothes, her combs and hairpins, some plates and plastic cups, were in place and perfectly clean she looked gratefully at Jamalat who had made everything shipshape and said to her: "God preserve you, Jamalat. By God, my spirit has been lifted."

Jamalat's round face broke into a gentle smile which made it look like the smiling face printed on children's sweet wrappers. She replied to Aziza saying: "Are you contented and happy then, love?"

Aziza cast her eye about the room once more with the kind of artificial disdain she usually displayed in the presence of those inferior to her – a legacy from her old life – then she was quiet for a little and said, "Get on and wash this plate and put it back in its place, then come and eat something to keep you going."

Jamalat went out to wash the plate still covered with leftovers which she had left in the communal washroom at the end of the long corridor near the ward. Meanwhile Aziza began to prepare Jamalat some bread and a piece of white cheese which Azima, the mourner, had given her with a Cleopatra cigarette – the not-for-export kind, rich with wood shavings. She also put aside a guava, one of four which 'Heroin Safiyya' had given her when sharing out amongst her friends and those she liked, a whole crate presented by her two sons on their last visit. She had not kept them for herself because she was afraid they might go off after a few days. As Aziza prepared the snack for Jamalat she began to think about the circumstances of the girl's life.

Jamalat returned and put the clean plate in the far corner of the room away from the bed and the clothes and then came to squat on the clean, swept floor next to Aziza. She placed the cheese on top of a flat loaf of bread and sank her teeth into it. Then as she chewed she said: "I want your opinion about something, Aunt Aziza".

"Is it something good?" Aziza replied enquiringly. Her eyes bulged as she fixed her gaze on Jamalat's angelic features because she thought Jamalat was going to draw her onto the subject of the golden winged chariot and her desire to join the ascent to heaven.

After she had finished the cheese, Jamalat pushed what was left of the bread into her mouth in one go. She shifted a piece of grit, which she came across in the last mouthful, to the front with her tongue and spat it out: "Do you know something . . . When I get out of here, God willing, after doing my time, I have been thinking about changing my job. Stealing has become more trouble than it's worth with all the rushing hither and thither so I've decided to work like girls from good families; I've had enough of all this strain and stress."

As she made this important statement Jamalat looked at Aziza wide-eyed and full of innocence. She had never confided her plan to anyone before but she trusted Aziza and felt at ease and secure with her despite all that was spread around the prison about her madness. For this reason she preferred to perform jobs for her rather than for the drug dealers who were excessively generous to those who waited on them and who used the considerable amounts of money they had to buy anything they wanted in prison, even bribing the warders. Although Jamalat sensed that Aziza was slightly mad because she sometimes looked at her in an unsettling way or smiled at her for no reason when they were chatting together, she still considered her a kind and sympathetic person who would always share anything she had. Jamalat had only to approach her about something for her to offer it to her, if it was within her power, and for this reason Jamalat ignored the rumours and warnings that Aziza might hit her or assault her if roused. Moreover Jamalat had found no one in the prison – a place where friendship between one prisoner and another was so vital – whom she would rather serve and be friends with than Aziza. They came to be like two sisters from the same womb, showing the same degree of sympathy and human understanding for each other. The ordeal of isolation and imprisonment behind bars created a bond between them which encouraged her to confide in Aziza her secret thoughts about what she intended to do if she managed to survive and get away from the place. Aziza was older and wiser and over time she had proved she was a good judge of character.

Aziza banged her head against the floor, thinking. The banging continued as Jamalat continued to put across her point of view clearly, although Aziza made no comment.

"Prostitution is easy and reliable and the sentences are light if you get caught by the police. If I stuck at it year after year I'd soon make a tidy sum of money after which my worries would be over. I would open a general hire shop which would earn enough for my daily sustenance, and that would be that."

Aziza did not reply because she was now fully engaged in watching a huge Persian ant dragging a tiny piece of bread which had fallen on the floor when Jamalat was eating a little while ago. It made its way towards its hiding place, a crack by the old door of the cell which was so scuffed that the dark wood showed through the paintwork. Aziza followed the ant intently with her eyes, announcing, "It would be better if you approached it from the top of the bed".

The ant responded by disappearing from sight into the crack. Jamalat, who had no idea what Aziza was on about, was busy tidying the fine strands of brown hair which had strayed onto her cheeks, and said, "You know . . . if they bring us some beef – I'm dying for a great fatty piece which I could boil and make a gravy out of vinegar and garlic – then you and I could sit and eat it together."

Aziza looked up from the floor and asked Jamalat to go and make some tea. When she stood up Aziza looked over her body, which was on the plump side, and her smooth white legs. She began to mull over what Jamalat had just told her, which was completely new to Aziza despite the long period they had been close friends in prison and all the details she already had of the girl's past and of why she had been imprisoned.

Aziza knew that Jamalat came from a family of gypsies whose skill as professional pickpockets and thieves had been passed down the generations. The men of the family practised their trade in Saudi Arabia and the Gulf, particularly during the pilgrimage season when the crowds provided an excellent source of income. Jamalat and her sister, who had no mother, lived where Jamalat's stealing took her – in the city of Tanta to be exact – especially during the festival of Saint Badawi when the crowds were at their height and everyone flocked to join in the festivities, providing ample opportunity for stealing.

However it was not stealing which finally led to Jamalat's arrest but a matter involving her sister who was about three years younger than her. She was more beautiful than Jamalat but was mentally retarded. She had suffered brain damage during a difficult birth, after which her mother died. She had softer hair than her elder sister and sweet, honey-coloured eyes, which attracted the attention of a young man who made advances to her. He had noticed that the two sisters lived on their own in a furnished apartment, a situation not considered socially acceptable, because of the way Egyptian cinema focused on the reputation of the inhabitants of these flats as being generally immoral and because of their connection to the world of oil money which had caused an increase in rental transactions as well as the related shady dealings which offended the law and religion. The problem arose because this simple-minded sister with her buxom body was more attracted to dairy products and sweets than she was to the young man; she was oblivious to the fact she was being pursued and he was totally unaware that she was simple-minded. Jamalat, who was alert to this, was afraid that one day this man would take advantage of her sister and that she would be faced with the added burden of having to feed three mouths instead of two. Her sister was a cross she had to bear day and night; she always accompanied her if she went out and, if she left her alone, she had to make sure that the windows were firmly secured and the front door double locked from the outside to prevent the foolish girl from letting someone in. Despite all these precautions, when Jamalat went out she was always apprehensive that her sister might expose herself to danger in her absence – that she would fiddle with a sharp tool or set fire to the house unintentionally.

Jamalat tried hard to encourage her sister to fend for herself and coached her in elementary stealing and simple methods of picking pockets. But this only compounded the problem. One day, she hurled the corn cob she was eating at the chest of an old man who was passing by, demanding that he empty his pockets of any money and hand it over to her. But for the fact that the old man thought it was the prank of a harmless young girl her action might have created no end of problems.

Jamalat warned the young man, who worked as an assistant in a hairdresser's shop on the ground floor of the block, that if he interfered with her sister she would give him such a beating that he would be no good to anyone. After begging him to keep away and to mind his own business, she was surprised one day to find the young man knocking on their door. When she opened up to insist that he should stop his foolish behaviour, which had reached the stage where he followed them to their front door, far from leaving and apologizing he pushed past her and forced his way inside. Before answering the door Jamalat had been ironing a red silk blouse, stolen from one of the most famous shops in the city, she unplugged the hot iron and hurled it at the young man. According to the doctors in the public hospital it had landed with full force on his head, causing severe concussion.

Aziza thought that Lula the hairdresser might have put Jamalat up to these new plans to become a prostitute, because Lula was a professional procuress who organized many networks of prostitutes, an activity which frequently landed her in prison. Amongst her victims were female university students, civil servants and middle class women. But Aziza pushed such thoughts from her mind because Jamalat loathed Lula and was always mocking her because she had found out that she preferred women to men. Everytime Lula had passed Jamalat standing in the prison courtyard she used to move up close to her without any good reason, and was eager to touch her in a peculiar way. In the beginning, Jamalat put this down to a display of friendship which made her happy because no one else showed her any sympathy or consideration. However, one day she went to wash in the prison bathroom; the water only trickled from the tap because about a month previously the stopcock had started leaking, so Jamalat asked Lula if she would fetch her a bucket of water. When she let her in to bring the water, Lula offered to massage her back with a loofah and soap. Once Lula started doing this it became clear to Jamalat that her real intention went beyond simply helping her to wash the parts of her body which were difficult to reach. Lula started breathing heavily as she praised the contours of Jamalat's body, which really was beautiful, despite being slightly on the plump side. Jamalat repelled these advances, needing no further proof of their immoral and shameful nature, but this did not deter Lula from spreading details of the episode to everyone in the prison, especially those who loved this sort of gossip like the old hags in the ward for the weak and of course Umm Ragab who spied for the authorities. The spreading of this slander was certainly to Lula's advantage, in that Saniya Matar, the most renowned drug dealer in the prison, sentenced to life for importing drugs by air from abroad, lapped up the news with the greatest glee and promptly included Lula in her list of favourites. However Jamalat continued to drip venom on Lula, poisoning the procuress's life. Lula felt angry and impotent in the face of this assault, and if she was unable to respond it was not through good manners or a virtuous tongue – neither her tongue nor the rest of her had ever been virtuous – but because, despite all the abuse and harsh words, she had really fallen in love with the young girl to the point of being unable to sleep.

At this point Aziza could not fathom what lay behind Jamalat's decision to change her way of life or what convinced her that it was the right thing to do because Aziza had not yet been introduced to Huda, the newest inmate of the scabies ward, who had arrived at the prison a week before. She was only sixteen years old, which made her the youngest woman in the whole prison, and she already had two babies. Despite her youth, it was she who had been able to convince Jamalat to pursue a new career which, Huda could testify from her own short but extensive experience of life, would be more lucrative.

Huda had landed in the gutter of depravity along a twisted path, which she never would have imagined possible. It had all started a few years back when she accompanied her mother to a police station for the first time, not because she was guilty of any crime but because her mother wanted to inform the police that one of her fourteen hens, which she had kept from the time they were chicks until they laid, had been killed. Huda's mother had accused a neighbour of the crime. The neighbour lived in a shack next to hers in one of the city suburbs which, over a few years, had swelled to resemble several large country towns. During the dispute with the tyrannical neighbour her mother received a direct blow with a large brick that ruptured her eye. A visit to the Government hospital followed, the purpose of which one might have guessed, was to get the eye examined. But not a bit of it, the real purpose of her mother's visit was to convince the extremely reluctant doctor on duty to issue a statement about the death of the assassinated hen, confirming that it had been killed by strangulation. She would then present this evidence to the police who could take the necessary steps against her neighbour.

The doctor failed to make Huda's mother understand that it was not his job to write medical reports on hens and when he offered to write a report certifying the serious damage she had suffered to her ruptured eye, she walked out in the belief that he was simply the stooge of a government which never got to the bottom of any problem. So she made for the police station and, once inside the door, met a distinguished staff sergeant who was not the least interested in the mother's lost eye, nor in the hen, the victim of this perfidious act, which was lying motionless, wrapped in part of the woman's long black scarf. All he was concerned with was sizing up the white, tender-skinned body of the young girl who was standing, clinging onto her mother and anxiously following what was going on around her. He brought them a cold drink – a most unusual thing to happen in a police station – and the mother became convinced that revenge would be meted out to her criminal enemy. He then asked her details about her daughter and after barely quarter of an hour had offered to marry the self same young girl standing beside her.

This momentous surprise made the mother forget about the eye she had lost, the wretched hen and the cruel neighbour. She had never in her wildest dreams imagined that she would become linked in any way to someone connected to the Government, especially someone so senior. It did not take long to agree to his proposal to marry her daughter, and her eyes gazed with amazement at the coloured badges fixed on his lapel which proved he was a staff sergeant and not a junior policeman without ribbons. She believed that destiny had crossed her path to pluck her from her utterly miserable life to better things. The man was generous and had made a serious offer, promising her a bridal dower of thirty pounds and the same value in clothes. He would include all the small necessities for a bride with a gold bracelet from Jamal, the jeweller, whose speciality was gold-plated copper jewellery, carrying the official hallmark, a guarantee particularly prized by poor peasants who were seldom able to afford such things.

Two months later the staff sergeant married the girl who was not yet thirteen years old. He managed to get round the legal age required for a girl to marry by purchasing a birth certificate for two pounds from a private doctor who also specialized in illegal medical activities like abortion and repairing the ruptured hymen of girls about to get married. Despite his conviction that the girl was under age, the official authorized to perform marriages agreed to write the contract. He was statisfied that the birth certificate, albeit forged, would deter any suspicious colleagues from causing trouble.

Only a year had gone by when Huda gave birth to a beautiful boy by the very same staff sergeant. The child was almost her double and by the time another year had passed there was a baby sister suckling beside him. However, her mother had become a chronic drug addict and passed on the addiction to her second child who was fretful and never stopped crying. Her addiction went back to the early days of their marriage when there wasn't a night when her husband returned without heroin or hashish which he usually obtained in raids on drug dealers or which the pushers in the quarter presented him with, to keep him sweet and to buy his silence. As time passed, the husband came home less and less and eventually abandoned his young family for another woman whom he met during his varied work. Huda had then to face life on her own, and to look for a means of supporting herself and her two children and, above all, of finding a way to meet the demands of a system accustomed to a daily intake of drugs. Necessity led her to reconsider her position and she took up the oldest and easiest profession in the world.

Jamalat was not in the scabies ward like Huda but because of their friendship she came to spend a major part of her time there. This was unlike most of the prisoners who avoided any contact with those who lived in that ward for fear of infection from the scabies brigade.

Because of their poverty these sufferers were unable to buy even a piece of the cheapest soap to wash themselves or their clothes, and had to make do with the tiny piece issued to them by the prison authorities. The full ration of soap which they should have received was lost in the pockets of the contractors and petty prison officials so most of these young bodies became a rich pasture on which the microscopic bugs could graze and settle permanently. It was Huda's zest for life, her good nature and her endless facility to crack jokes that attracted Jamalat to her as well as the dancing and singing sessions which they both joined in with the rest of the girls on the ward. Huda tried very hard, albeit unsuccessfully, to imitate the voice of Farid El-Atrash, whom she adored, but was still the unrivalled star of the concerts in the scabies ward, despite her youth. Everyone felt bound to obey her orders, particularly the rotas for sleeping places and cleaning tasks – although the latter were extremely limited due to the almost complete lack of cleaning materials. During the day Huda also saw to the collection of old bits of paper and rags from the prison courtyard which were burnt at night in an unsuccessful attempt to get rid of the mosquitoes. These mosquitoes vied with the awful scabie bugs in sucking the blood of the prisoners; the smoke rising from the fire was insufficient to deter the mosquitoes and merely caused chest complaints.

Aziza lit up a cigarette, and thought sadly: if Jamalat becomes one of those who sell their bodies to any man who can pay, how many men will taste the nectar of this tender body seated before me? Aziza thought of the old men, the tall men, the short men and those with huge paunches and teeth, discoloured and rotten through drug-taking, who might squeeze the last bloom of youth from Jamalat's body and would completely destroy her spirit reducing her to a human rag, worn out from over-use. She asked herself why it was ordained that a beautiful young girl like her should have to put up with all this ugliness and why her life, which had hardly started, should take such a course which could only lead to a dead end. Why shouldn't Jamalat find a man who was as good as her, to whom she could give herself body and soul and who would give her everything a man can give a woman? Her thoughts raced ahead, imagining what would happen if Jamalat were to do what she was thinking of. She would then undoubtedly become another Lula, an experienced procuress not content with selling her own body but also engaged in selling the bodies of others.

This line of thought not only made Aziza sad but extremely angry as well. She lifted her head and fixed her eyes on the iron bars of the window and let out a cry of protest directed towards an undefined and supreme force which she considered responsible for all that had happened and would happen in the future to this decent, lovely girl with her pure heart and childlike innocence. All the while she peered upwards at a chink of blue sky, cloaked by dark grey clouds, sadly saying: "Can you hear? Can you see? Things have gone too far to be ignored any longer." Then she continued with a note of defiance in her voice:

"Very well, and on my mother's soul, this girl will come up with us, God willing, and she will sit right next to me. The first step must be to give her a hot bath with fenugreek soap to guard against infection and to ensure she is beautiful and lovely for the journey."

At that moment, Jamalat, who had been busy scratching the infection between her fingers, became aware that Aziza was talking. She turned to where she was standing in the corner of the room and poured the tea into two glasses on a tray; she had delayed pouring it out until it had turned a dark ruby-red colour. Then turning to Aziza she addressed her in a puzzled way, calling her by the special name she used when she was in a good mood:

"Did you say something, moonbeam?"

5

Mercy before Justice

As Mahrousa, the prison warder, lifted her head from a plate of honey, Safiyya the heroin addict began to massage the warder's face to stop the honey from dripping. After removing the hair and fine down growing round the chin, cheeks and bridge of her nose with some plaited thread, she washed it in water without soap. Having removed these blemishes she was well pleased with the softness and glow on Mahrousa's face.

Mahrousa smiled at the thought of her face after this treatment and, in a hoarse voice, she began to sing a joyous wedding song, remembered from the days of her youth some thirty years ago. Then she said, sighing sadly: "You know my dear Safiyya, when I was in the full flush of my youth my skin was so beautiful and smooth that a love bird could have picked up a crumb from it!"

"Amazing!" replied Safiyya, adding, "Worry and sadness is enough to wreck anyone in this life – even someone as beautiful as Badr al-Bandour – and you have certainly had your fair share of ups and downs, may God help you."

Mahrousa pursed her lips and her face looked even more swollen than usual after the plucking. She sighed deeply and began a well-known mournful song: "The book of my life, my love . . . la, la la."

Then she stopped singing and began to speak,

"You know, if anyone else had gone through what I have and experienced life in the way I have, they would probably have committed suicide and died an unbeliever. By God, such is their right but, thank God, my heart is as pure as the white scarf wrapped around your head, Safiyya, and I have sought nothing but good for people. God rewards everyone according to his merits."

Safiyya agreed, saying, "You are right . . . God awards you your just deserts." Safiyya reminded her of the incident involving the murderess, Samiha who stole a bit of a broken fenugreek bottle from the prison hospital and hid it amongst her things. She intended to use it as a weapon during the endless battles with the other prisoners and was caught out by Mahrousa quite by chance. Safiyya praised her good heart because if any other prison warder had discovered such an offence the prisoner would have been in deep trouble with the prison authorities who would have imposed a heavy punishment. What's more, if Samiha had used this dangerous weapon, the authorities could have had a tragedy on their hands. Mahrousa was satisfied that slapping her across her ugly face was enough to put the fear of God into anyone, and sufficient to make Samiha mend her evil ways. Mahrousa swore by her mother in heaven that if Samiha engaged in any further activities which went against the prison rules there would be no alternative but to bind her hands and feet and pinch her with two dry date pits on the tender area of her thighs. This treatment, which was immensely painful and left the soft areas of skin severely bruised, was the very same deterrent that Mahrousa had often employed against her daughters if they did something serious which deserved a harsher punishment than the more usual slap.

Mahrousa's heart wasn't white like the prison scarf Safiyya was wearing, it was black like a cold wintry night overcast with clouds without a single shining star to lighten the gloom. The sun never rose in Mahrousa's heart to erase the black hatred which had settled there over time. This hatred was directed against people, life, time and, above all else, her husband, because he as good as killed her when she was in her prime and left her to shoulder all the responsibilities after stealing everything she owned. This included the gold she received when she married and the only piece of jewellery she possessed, an eighteen carat gold ring with a small carnelian red stone. He also stole her household effects which she had collected bit by bit, sweating blood as a housemaid from sunrise until well beyond sunset to make a living for him and their children and for which she received nothing in return but a broken heart. This husband had not an ounce of mercy and even told her once that he hated her because she was ugly and misshapen – or rather she was the ugliest woman ever created on the face of this earth.

Poor tormented Mahrousa was only too aware of this truth which her faithless husband had confronted her with. She admitted that she was ugly and deformed, with her wide face, snub nose and bulging frog-like eyes which were in no way mitigated by her dark, almost bluish, lack-lustre skin and her wide mouth poised above her huge ball-shaped chin. However, it was one thing for her to be aware of this truth and quite another to be told this by her husband and the father of her children – indeed by the person closest to her heart. The moment she heard it she suffered such pain that it consumed her soul and crushed her spirit. She knew that there was nothing that could be done and that she would never be beautiful because the way she looked was in the hands of fate, but she longed to be acceptable at least, with a normal face like other people. She continued to dye her hair with henna, becoming an expert; sometimes she would knead the henna in boiling water with the skins of black aubergine and golden red onions from the country; at other times she added camomile and black tea, diluted after boiling it for some time. She took equal pains to keep her body soft, using any beauty preparations she could get hold of. Sometimes she bought these and at other times she was given them by the women whose houses she cleaned. One thing she had a problem with was peeling nail varnish which was inevitable since the domestic work she did meant immersing her hands in water most of the time.

What hurt Mahrousa most about her husband was that he never appreciated the extraordinary efforts she made to be beautiful; nor did he ever thank her for the financial contribution she made. No matter how tired she was, he insisted on having sex with her every night which resulted in half-a-dozen children – four girls and two boys. She never once heard a kind word from him and because he suffered from a lung complaint, she never felt able to refuse him intercourse. She waited on him hand and foot because she believed that illness and good health are in God's hands and that He, in His wisdom, decides who is destined to have one or the other. So she continued to obey this cruel husband, believing it to be a divine obligation, tantamount to obedience to God. In this way she cared for him, providing half a litre of milk especially for him daily. She brought back the best food she could lay her hands on from the rich houses where she worked – the kind of food they could never afford to make at home – and fed him on it, stinting herself. Her husband was a labourer who teased out compacted cotton with a wire bow to use for the padding in upholstery. The dust which rose up from the cotton stuffing and the old mattresses began to affect his chest until his condition became chronic and he was forced to stop working. He then sat at home, a lump of living flesh with no work and nothing to do. Even then Mahrousa continued to spend her money on him, handing him cash so that he could sit in cafés like other men who were still earning their living and had not been struck down by ill-health. She wanted to spare him the anguish of feeling like a bird with a broken wing, debilitated by illness which had denied him his proper role as breadwinner for his family.

But her husband met this kindness and thoughtfulness with rejection and cruelty. He upbraided her harshly for the smallest involuntary lapses which only happened through pressure of time or exhaustion: one evening she was so tired that she threw herself on the mattress and fell asleep after switching off the stove before the soured milk had had time to boil. As a result it curdled and when her husband discovered that it had gone off he swore at her using the most despicable words, even cursing her father and grandfather. But none of these abuses hurt her as much as the way he called her a body which had been dumped on him and wasn't worth a penny in the market. After that he began to hit her and the children for the slightest thing, finally accusing her of immoral behaviour because she came home late from work. God knows that the only reason she stayed out late was to complete her work to perfection in order to earn the approval of her employers and avoid being sacked; working overtime also earned her more money to feed her family. Mahrousa endured these insults and accepted her destiny, which would protect and safeguard her, believing that it was better to be married than to live alone. However her anxiety increased when her husband changed his tactics and began to steal from her. One evening she came home exhausted from working late, having recently taken on cleaning the apartment of an important merchant. It had six rooms, an enormous fully-equipped kitchen full of gadgets and three bathrooms where she religiously cleaned and polished all the tiled surfaces. On her return she discovered that her husband had taken the television and sold it for a trifling sum. The television had provided the rare moments of happiness in her life when she snuggled up with her children at suppertime, to watch the plays and films. She would fall asleep on the sofa in front of the television, dreaming she was one of the blonde, white-skinned girls in the advertisements who wore such pretty dresses and whom the men raved about. So devastated was she by this blow that she lost her appetite; she had dreamed of owning a television for ages and finally bought one from a good lady whose husband had brought a large new television back from one of his trips abroad. It was a real bargain and she had been allowed to pay for it in instalments.

After the saga of the television came the black day when, as far as Mahrousa was concerned, the sun never rose. On this day the washing machine disappeared. You can imagine the scale of the disaster if I tell you that she considered washing machines the greatest invention on earth. Her washing machine released her from the slavery of washing her family's clothes; the value she placed on it and the reverence she showed towards it was obvious from the way she dried it carefully each time she used it and draped it with a beautiful coloured scarf, one of the occasional items she had been given by her employers.

On that unhappy day she did not restrain herself as she had on the day her husband sold the television but faced him with the truth that he was always gambling at cards in the café with the rogues of the quarter. Then she cried bitterly over the demise of her beloved washing machine, just as any poor peasant mourns the death of his buffalo, the mainstay of his life. She cursed her bad luck and invoked her long departed mother to come to her aid and witness the calamity that had befallen her. This washing machine had been a windfall which Mahrousa believed could never be replaced; she had bought it one day from a rag and bone man doing his rounds. She guessed that the machine, which was as good as new, must have been stolen and after a lengthy discussion as to how much it was worth, who it was made by and so on, she ended up paying only thirty pounds for it from her hard-earned savings.

After suffering many years of torment with her sick husband, the gambler and sadist, he deserted her and completely disappeared, but not before robbing her of her only piece of jewellery which, as far as she was concerned, was as valuable as King Solomon's treasure and her only security against hard times. He stole the ring from her finger in the dead of night when she was stretched out like a corpse, fast asleep before the dawn of another exhausting day. She had come across the ring, which had a fake carnelian stone, quite by chance in the inside pocket of an old coat belonging to a Greek lady she worked for. She had been presented with the coat when the lady was forced to leave quickly when in 1956 foreigners were expelled from the country.

After he deserted her Mahrousa abandoned all hope of her errant husband ever returning. She was forced to move around from job to job because domestic work was no longer easy to find. The spread of electrical appliances and the tendency to choose practical furnishings enabled people to manage the daily chores on their own and dispense with servants.

At first Mahrousa took up cooking *kushari* made from rice, noodles, lentils, fried onions and spicey sauce which she sold on the pavement. But as soon as she managed to get back on her feet and save a little money she was pursued by municipal officials, demanding protection money and fees which which she was forced to pay in order to get the necessary licence to ply her trade in peace. The pavements were the property of the Government who doled out licences to traders on a purely arbitrary basis. Mahrousa decided she had had enough of selling *kushari* after she discovered that the financial return was negligible; the taxes and bribes she was forced to pay exceeded her earnings and after she had paid off the wholesaler for the noodles, lentils and rice, which she bought on credit, at the end of the day she made no profit at all.

After that she went into 'manufacturing', perhaps spurred on by the general trend of the 'open-door' economic policy which was meant to promote manufacturing but failed to build the factories to make the goods. The scale of Mahrousa's industrial plans differed considerably. She started picking up any discarded paper she could find on the street, thrown out by import-export dealers, and used them to make clowns' hats and paper fans. She fixed these onto sticks made from stripped palm branches, used to make cages, which had ended up on the rubbish dump in the market. She stuck the hats and fans onto the sticks with starch made from cooked rice then, in order to paint them, she boiled up left-over vegetables and scraps to make dyes which were brightly coloured to attract children. Then, in this attempt to stave off destitution, she roamed the markets and saints' day festivals, selling her wares for a few pennies.

During this critical period of her life, a neighbour enticed her to work with him in a Punch and Judy show. Her husky voice was projected from behind the curtain and she played the part of the mother-in-law who is always stirring up trouble and dissension between her daughter and hen-pecked husband. Apart from her main role she also sang some ditties which brought laughter and mockery from the audience. Mahrousa found this work easy and was happy because it did not sap her strength or undermine her health, which had recently deteriorated. Chronic rheumatism had spread to her joints despite the fact that her work-load, apart from the show, was light and only involved cooking and occasional washing for her employer.

She was esctatic about her new role in the Punch and Judy show because it made her feel loved by people, especially children, who laughed uproariously and screamed when it was her turn to sing. At last she was accepted after feeling alienated for so long, and earning a wage was an additional bonus. Her work was eventful to say the least: one day the owner of a large café surprised her by inviting them to give a show for a circumcision party. This was to be on behalf of a prosperous man whose son had been born after seven daughters, produced by three different wives; only the last wife had enabled him to fulfil his dream of producing the son from his loins who would succeed him and preserve his name for posterity.

Mahrousa made her mark in her new role and even contributed new ideas of her own; to the delight of her audience she told riddles, usually during the intervals. By extending the performance she was also able to attract bigger crowds and thus earn more money. A typical riddle she asked them might be: "What crosses the sea without drowning?" – and by the sea she knew the people understood she was referring to the River Nile. It was common to use this terminology and indicated the reverence and affection felt for this great river. One of the more witty members of the audience might then give the answer: "A buffalo calf in its mother's stomach because a buffalo can easily float in the Nile, even when pregnant", at which point Mahrousa would ask the audience to applaud this intelligent response while Punch played one of Hasab Allah's famous melodies by way of congratulation. Mahrousa would go on to deliver the second of four riddles which were the only ones she knew, asking her audience: "What hovers over a glass plate?" Then she got to the third riddle, which she considered the most difficult of all, which went like this: "A container within another container immersed in water; inside it are pearls and its outside is copper coloured. What is it?" At this stage the audience would inevitably give the wrong answer but Mahrousa gave them more time to think during which she would circulate, collecting money. Only when she returned to Punch would she tell them the answer which was: "A pomegranate". Then she would throw out the last one which was: "Something which shines and glistens and hides between leaves." Then she would join with Punch in the second part of the show which followed this interval.

However, not long after, Mahrousa had to leave the work that she loved so much. She was astounded when the very man who played Punch, made it clear that he not only wanted to have sex with her but also wanted her to do it with other men. He was most insistent that she agree to both demands, planning to share with her the income she earned from prostitution in return for his protection and procurement of men for her.

After she left the Punch and Judy group Mahrousa and her children went through dark times. She was forced to beg in the streets to stave off the hunger of six little mouths which were constantly open, demanding food. She found work with removal men and her hopes were raised only to be dashed when she injured the vertebrae in her lower back. As if this wasn't enough, one night she was returning from her work in an apartment far out in one of the new suburbs of Masr Jadida, when she was raped by three soldiers, the same age as her eldest daughter. After gagging her and binding her with their army belts the gang raped her, leaving her in such a state that she would never know how she managed to get home. In the days that followed, Mahrousa rummaged around in dustbins for anything fit to eat. She got hold of some offal and discarded remains from a man who slaughtered and sold chickens which she stewed and gave to her children with bread. But God was to intervene and show mercy to this wretched woman. One happy day one of her husband's relatives, who was working as a staff sergeant in the prisons, was unexpectedly transfered to the women's prison. Having just heard that she had been abandoned by his relation and witnessed the misery and deprivation that she and her children had suffered, he went out and bought a tin of *halawa* made from the best ground sesame seed and syrup, some flat loaves of white bread and a packet of tea which he sat and shared with them. Then after slipping three pounds into Mahrousa's hand, which were the only notes he had left in his pocket, he promised to try and find her a job which would give her a regular income and save her from begging on the streets. Hardly a month went by before Mahrousa was wearing the warder's uniform, a blue-grey overall; she was appointed because the authorities were impressed by her hefty size and the forbidding look in her eye that gave her a stern appearance, both of which, in their view, qualified her for the new post.

Despite the extraordinary experiences and suffering Mahrousa had already encountered in her life, her job opened her eyes to a world of human relationships wholly outside her previous experience; with the turnover of prisoners she was constantly exposed to new stories of tragedy. She became aware of the comforting truth that she wasn't the only oppressed woman in the world as she had thought, nor was she alone in suffering from misfortune; there were many other women to whom fate had dealt a terrible blow and had robbed of happiness and mercy. In her new profession she was required to be firm, strict and authoritative which gradually gave her self-confidence and strength but this neither eliminated the blackness in her heart nor nor banished the bitterness from her soul. The lasting feelings of failure and the sense of an absence of justice in life which she harboured made her compassionate in her dealings with the prisoners. She was sympathetic to their plight, and had reached the conclusion that mercy should always come before justice; there was no hope for the human race without mercy which, if allowed to surface in human relations, would go some way towards eradicating misery in life. For this reason she was honest with the prisoners and didn't oppress or exploit them. She didn't impose fines on them like some of the other warders nor did she expect them to render services for her without anything in return; even when Safiyya, the heroin addict, made her a crochet shawl she reciprocated by giving her a whole chicken which she had boiled herself at home and brought to the prison. She was also quite happy to accept presents from the prisoners on condition that they offer them freely and without expecting any special favour in return. On this basis she accepted the honey in which her face had been immersed a short time ago from a prisoner whose family owned a large number of hives in their village. Generally she would only stretch out her hand to accept something from the prisoners after satisfying herself that, weighed on the scales of justice, the gift had come through the door of love, mercy and compassion, all qualities necessary to survive the terrible life in prison.

The reasons behind the special relationship between Mahrousa and Safiyya, nicknamed 'Heroin Safiyya' on account of her predeliction for this kind of drug, were different from those linking her to all the other prisoners. Time, above all else, had played a part in forging this relationship because Safiyya had served a longer time in prison than anyone else. More significantly, she was the most generous and experienced in prison affairs because she had spent most of her life there, arriving for the first time at the age of sixteen sentenced to a year for stealing. When she was nineteen she joined a gang of armed robbers and was sent down for six years with hard labour. When she got out she married one of her relations who was unemployed but had an apartment with a reception room and two bedrooms which he had inherited from his mother. This provided a haven of rest and shelter. At this stage she sold a gold watch which she had kept for herself, never owning up to the fact that it was stolen when she was arrested, and with the proceeds bought herself a cheap shirt from a textile merchant in al-Azhar street and plastic house slippers for almost nothing. She also purchased artificial necklaces, bracelets and earings to form a modest stock in trade which she resold to women on her rounds of the apartment blocks and houses. Gradually, trade increased thanks to her industry and the good use she made of her charm and experience to build her customers' confidence in her. She expanded her activities into several new areas: for some of the women she made a lemon and sugar paste to remove body hair; she made blankets and head scarves out of crocheted wool; she blended oils for the skin and hair, having obtained the ingredients and formulae from perfume makers. Finally she began to offer a special service, preparing brides for their wedding night. Everything she offered was performed to perfection and she became greatly in demand. She reached the stage where she had many customers, none of whom knew anything about her criminal past, and her circumstances improved so greatly that she was able to live a pleasant existence of a kind she could have never dreamed of in her previous life.

After Safiyya had been married for five years, she gave birth to twin boys whom she was crazy about despite the fact that they were extremely skinny and their heads were squashed in at the back. She considered them the greatest of earth's creations and now that she had a family to care for she felt a sense of belonging for the first time. After she had lost her real father she had spent a miserable childhood with her stepfather, finally running away from home when she was fourteen. She had left her country village in the Delta, and travelled to Cairo only to end up wandering aimlessly about the streets, day after day, begging for sustenance. This went on until she caught the eye of the owner of a scalding house who noticed her loitering near his shop in the souk. She began to work with him, cleaning the stomachs of cattle and sheep, washing away the filth by immersing them in boiling water. When she had finished this first task she had to clean the aluminium cups and plates used for serving sopped bread, meat and broth to the customers. In return for this work Safiyya was given food and a place in the kitchen to rest her head late at night.

The truth was that Safiyya was lucky since she had escaped the trials experienced by other youngsters on the run in a city as hellish as

Cairo. This luck was not due to divine intervention nor to any lack of wolves waiting to trap an unsuspecting female who crossed their path in the city, but was rather the result of a natural immunity: Safiyya only had one eye. She had lost her other eye a long time ago when she tried to escape a violent thrashing from her stepfather for breaking the long-necked bottle of his water-pipe while carrying it to him for his midday smoke. At that moment her mother had been busy making a woollen skull cap for her husband, embellishing it with a zig-zag, wave-like design used by the ancient Egyptians and meant to represent the River Nile. In order to escape the rage of her stepfather, the wretched child ran to hide in her mother's lap, falling onto the steel sewing needle which sank into her eye and tore it out. After that she had one eye which she could see with and the other which was glass. This was provided by her stepfather who was decent enough to feel responsible for the little girl's accident. Although he really hated and disliked having anything to do with the child, he had never intended to hurt her in a way which could lead to her losing the sight of an eye. Safiyya's glass eye was not the only natural immunity she possessed against being raped; she was extremely weak and skinny and her lack of any experience in matters feminine was extremely off-putting. When she was fourteen she looked about eight; she was short, virtually flat-chested with a tiny head and a chin which looked as if it came straight out of her shoulders. Perhaps this explains why, when she asked for a train ticket from the Delta to Cairo the man let her off, sitting quietly, as she was, next to an old peasant, gazing with her one eye at the countryside rolling past her with its villages, and fields full of cotton and vegetables. Even the first incident she faced, which could at a stretch be described as 'rape', concerned a boy who was years younger than her and in no way mature. At noon one day during the *al-Fitr* festival at the end of the fasting month of Ramadan, she went to the cinema decked out in a new shift of velvet winceyette, with brightly-coloured rabbits, geese and cocks printed on it. This had been presented by the owner of the scalding house who also chose some fabric shoes with rubber soles and bows, in a colour which would not show the dirt. These shoes were of the kind marketed throughout the city by the Italian factories which had sprung up all over the place and had eventually been nationalized. He also gave

Safiyya the princely sum of ten piasters, as a special bonus to spend over the three-day festival. She thanked him profusely and grasped both his plump hands, planting copious kisses on them. She bought some *falafel*, and some *fuul* with *tahina* to mix together – a combination which was almost musical in its harmony. As she was finishing it off, she walked along gazing at the shops and stalls, and some red plastic earings caught her eye; she immediately fell for them and bought them for two piasters. The film showing at the cinema featured a singer and a famous belly dancer; the movement of the dancer's bare stomach and chest as well as the rest of her body called for the greatest skill, particularly below the waist. As she watched Safiyya felt a hand grope across to her chest and fondle her breasts; the pleasure she felt as it reached the tips of her little nipples kept her quiet, and she imagined herself as Alice in Wonderland as she watched the film with her single eye. The long hand which stretched towards her from the next door seat, continued to grope her, jumping to another area of her little body, arousing feelings of pleasure she had never experienced before.

Events moved on when the lights were suddenly turned on at the start of a short interval, the idea of which was to enable the usher to sell fizzy drinks, peanuts and sunflower seeds to the audience. When Safiyya looked round there was no one on the seat next to her. The boy had made off in a hurry, perhaps because he was embarrassed when the lights came on or possibly because he had quickly glanced at her face and noticed the glass eye. She gave up hope of his returning and bought herself a Pepsi because she felt so thirsty.

As time passed Safiyya turned into a Cairene girl; her eyes were opened to the marvels and excitement of life in a metropolis which was like many cities rolled into one. When her boss sent her on errands for himself or other traders in the souk, she took advantage of these occasions away from the scalding house. She wandered about the streets, lingering in front of the window displays of the large stores and watching upper class women who whiled away their mornings shopping, avidly purchasing goods to stave off boredom. At this moment in her life, Safiyya's ultimate dream was to obtain some red shoes with high heels, a dream she was able to realize two months later thanks, not entirely to luck, but because she was sharp and light-fingered. While she was passing by a shoe mender's she noticed two small red shoes lying, one on top of the other, next to a pile of shoes waiting to be mended. She was so taken with them that she dreamed that very night of her stepfather who kissed the shoes and stroked her face with them before slipping her feet into them. The next day the image of the red shoes remained vividly before her, and she thought up a mischievous plan which would help her achieve what she wanted. She took one of her employer's shoes after he had removed it to perform the evening prayer, and when he wasn't looking, sliced off the sole with a sharp knife. When he had finished his praying, adding two extra prostrations to ask God for righteousness and success, he slipped his foot into the shoe only to discover that there was nothing between his toes and the floor except his wine-red socks. This infuriated him and he started to curse the shoe industry and the swindlers who owned it, swearing that he would never buy another shoe from the shop where he had bought this one. Safiyya, meanwhile, tried to calm him down and rushed off with the shoe to the shoe menders, promising him that she would return only when the shoe was restored to its former condition and that it was pointless giving himself high blood pressure and getting himself in a state.

She returned an hour later with three shoes rather than one, including the red pair she had coveted and even dreamed of. She had worked hard to convince the shoe mender of the urgency of mending her employer's shoe by duping him into believing that she worked as a servant for some important official and his wife who mistreated her, and would undoubtedly hit her if she didn't return quickly. The man felt sorry for her when he heard the story of what her stepfather had done to her and saw her glass eye and was moved by the pathetic way she begged him to help. So he sent her off to buy him some fried aubergines and potatoes for lunch and when he had finished eating she brought him a glass of tea from the nearby café which he drank while mending the shoe. As soon as he finished restoring the shoe to its former glory the man went to the lavatory above the shop to relieve himself and this gave Safiyya the perfect opportunity to grab hold of the red shoes. She quickly snatched the single shoe he had just finished mending, as well as the red shoes, and flew like a little sparrow out of the shop and back to the scalding house.

When she returned she discovered that the heels of the red shoes were still broken but their acquisition nevertheless marked a glorious new stage in her dreary existence which before had been empty of any kindness and joy. She was so poor that she was unable to buy anything she wanted and this train of thought awakened her for the first time to an important truth: the owner of the scalding house who had rescued her from misery and who, until now, she had considered heaven sent, was in fact exploiting her terribly. She worked daily from six in the morning until after nightfall without a break, except for a short pause after lunch. In return for this she received just enough to avoid starvation – a little piece of sheep's trotter or sheep's head, with a plate of rice to which some broth had been added. This meagre ration sometimes forced her to eat the leftovers from customers' plates, although it was only seldom that they left any food. In addition to this she was given a glass or two of tea daily and stole any other food she was able to, like fruit which she took when delivering some to her employer's wife. She longed to have her hair styled and to fasten it with a band of coloured pearls, to put on red lipstick to match her red shoes like the city women did. When she saw them, anger and exasperation welled up inside her against the owner of the scalding house who was exploiting her and thwarting her plans. She then came to an important conclusion: as far as she was concerned, stealing in this city was not only feasible and extremely simple but essential if you wanted to live your life as many people walking the streets did.

After this episode and well beyond, the importance of the scalding house diminished in Safiyya's eyes – or rather the one which was not made of glass – and it became just a matter of time before she left. The call of the city beckoned, offering her untold joys on condition that she made use of her wits and her light-fingered touch; thus she became one of its villains who lived by thieving as long as circumstances permitted.

While Safiyya remained at the scalding house she could only steal small items which were easy to hide. Soon after the episode of the red shoes – which were of little cash value – she managed to collect a large number of cheap earrings, hair combs, hairpins and men's and women's socks which she stole from pedlars displaying their cheap goods on the pavements. After a period she discovered that there were rich pickings to be made from lovers who went to the cinema, especially those who came out of the nine o'clock performance, still intoxicated by the passionate scenes they had watched, identifying with the hero or beautiful heroine in the film. The ardent kisses they stole from each other in the dark were still on their lips and it was easy for Safiyya to rob them of the fine chiffon scarves which dangled ostentatiously from the elegant handbags or key rings which hung from the trouser pockets of flash young men. The fact that she was so tiny made the chances of catching her much smaller.

One black day, which she would never forget, she unwittingly fell into the clutches of the police and, to that day, she had never regretted anything so much as the carelessness and recklessness which led her to make such a mistake. It was about three months after she had reached puberty and she was walking along the streets of the city, exhausted. She was suffering from her period which made every bone of her body ache as if she were about to fall apart, when she caught sight of a woman with a huge behind like most Egyptian women have, accompanied by a little girl about six years old. The child was wearing a gold chain around her neck with a blue-jewelled pendant. They were wandering about looking at children's clothes when they suddenly stopped in front of a shop window. The mother was busy examining the goods on display with a view to choosing something for her child when Safiyya stretched out her hand from behind to reach for the clasp of the necklace resting on the girl's neck, and tried to open it. However, the little girl noticed immediately and screamed, at which point her mother turned round, roughly grabbed hold of Safiyya's hand and called for help from passers-by.

By a stroke of bad luck the woman was the daughter of a senior police officer and so Safiyya was singled out for a harsh beating. She was handed over to police officers experienced in techniques of torture which do not leave traces that could be used as evidence by government doctors investigating allegations of brutality. When they had completed their business, which lasted almost an hour, Safiyya felt that her left eye must surely have suffered the same damage that had been inflicted on her right eye all those years ago. The next day she came before the prosecuting authorities who referred her case to the courts. She received a year's prison sentence, the first of many, which was to mark the beginning of a long-drawn out association between Safiyya and prison, her new companion for life.

It seemed as if fate had lain in wait for Safiyya, in the same way that it maintains its grip on all human affairs, despite the efforts individuals make to control their destiny and live in uninterrupted peace and contentment. There are some people whose future is mapped out for them from the moment they are born; Safiyya's life had never gone smoothly. Even when she found happiness with her sons and her husband, a pillar of strength who was happier caring for the children and doing the housework than working in a job outside, she was forced to leave them. The competence and love with which he cared for the children left Safiyya free to pursue her vital task bringing in the family income. She provided them with everything they needed and was determined to fulfil the dream she shared with her husband to send the boys to university – a dream held by thousands of the poor after Nasser announced free education for all. Safiyya and her husband believed that higher education was the only way to become respected in society – a hope they cherished more than any other for their children. For this reason Safiyya worked ceaselessly to provide her boys with the same material advantages enjoyed by more privileged families; she was keen that their clothes should be smart and their house clean and full of all the modern equipment which reflected breeding and refinement so that her two boys could compete on equal terms with their friends. She bought everything regardless of cost or whether it was practical or necessary, such as a gas igniter, insect repellents and air fresheners in aerosol cans. She bought various different kinds of shampoo, an electric hair-dryer, as well as major electrical appliances like a washing machine, refrigerator, cooker, television and a video. With almost tragic ease, and driven by the expectations of her happy family caught up in a consumer society which craves the latest of everything, Safiyya entered the world of Tafida, the biggest drug dealer in the notorious "red route district".

Tafida considered Safiyya a rare type in her wide trading network, a precisely-tuned organization which escaped raids from the police. The latter were extremely well acquainted with Tafida's activities but, because she ran her organization so skilfully, they were unable to gather sufficient evidence to convict her; besides, many of those who were paid to watch her used their eyes to watch for her as well. Tafida benefited greatly from Safiyya's wide network of connections and acquaintances which she had built up through her frequent comings and goings to people's houses and was still able to cultivate without arousing any suspicion. She undertook the difficult task of distributing the drugs in return for a much greater sum than she had earned from trading in fabric and other little goods. Her financial circumstances improved substantially so that she was able to buy a shop for her husband and two sons. This became an outlet for selling trashy American videos full of violence and karate, as well as Egyptian films which were useless. By a stroke of ill fate, the owner of the glass eye happened to come under the scrutiny of the police while she was distributing some heroin to one of Tafida's drug pushers who lived in a city suburb. The police happened to be raiding the same apartment block where the dealer was living to arrest a member of one of the Islamic groups. They combed through the block searching for bombs, explosives and various incendiary devices used by such groups against the authorities. The police left no stone unturned as they conducted their search with enthusiasm and precision in an apartment block which was considered a prime example of the demise of Cairo's architectural heritage. This block resembled a shoe box standing on its end, with openings and windows, and painted in colours devoid of any sense of taste or beauty making the front of the building look like a slice of sickly confectionary. It was a testimony to the absence of any conscience on the part of municipal workers and local mayors when they carried out such building projects, as well as the monopoly of the dealers in cement and reinforced iron and the rogues who called themselves builders or architects in the construction sector. It was Safiyya's bad luck that the police searched the fine chamois handbag; she had been carrying it under her arm in a manner not entirely in keeping with a woman who had a glass eye and a body which wasn't much bigger than the bag. They ordered her to open it and found pouches full of powdered drugs waiting for them, lying pressed together under a piece of coloured material, men's socks and silk ties, all imported through the free port at Port Said.

In this way, Safiyya returned to prison with no particular feelings of despair, unlike previous occasions. She was well satisfied with herself for fulfilling her ultimate aim to send the two boys to university; the first was doing extremely well in agricultural studies but like many others abandoned agriculture after graduation to join the world of tourism, property dealing, middlemen and people who call themselves "businessmen". Safiyya managed to secure a reasonable income for the two boys, enough to enable the second boy to get engaged to a university friend whom he loved and was determined to marry.

Another reason why Safiyya was not particularly upset about returning to prison on this occasion was that she had converted most of her gains from drug dealing into gold jewellery. Some time before her arrest she had bought a plot of land in which she buried the jewellery safely beneath two graves, erected specially for this purpose and which she surrounded with high walls. The entrance was made secure by a huge wrought-iron gate, the key of which she resolved never to entrust to the gravedigger as a precaution against government interference. She had been warned that they intended to confiscate her possessions, fixed and moveable, thereby eroding everything which had been built through the sweat of her brow, through legal and illegal means.

Safiyya was sentenced to life imprisonment but she thanked God since shortly after her case the death penalty was imposed for drug pushers and smugglers. However the rigour of prison life began to take its toll and time weighed heavily on her, hastening her entry into the fellowship of the aged. She was tormented by the thought that she would die alone, far from her two boys and that she would never be able to live with them again. She spent her nights thinking about them and shed many tears for them; even when she was overcome by sleep she continued to talk to them in her dreams – the happiest moments in her prison life – as if she were still living with them. She cautioned her second son against spoiling his fiancée too much lest she become full of herself and create problems for him. She helped the first one, who was colour-blind, choose his clothes, particularly as he was unable to distinguish between blue and green. As for her second husband, she remembered him with affection because he was the only man in the world who had taken her into his arms and protected her. She had met him by chance when she wrote to her mother one day in the far off village where she lived, at a time when she was out of prison and was carrying on a lucrative business. Her mother replied with the news of her first husband's death, giving her the address of a relation in Cairo with whom she went to stay. When he found that she was generous, would not be a burden on him and that what was hers would also be his, he told himself that he could only gain by marrying her and that given his difficult circumstances, it was unlikely he would find a better wife.

As time dragged by in prison, Safiyya became increasingly exasperated and angry with the Government which she saw as the cause of all her problems and unhappiness and her separation from her family. She didn't understand, and nor would she ever understand, why someone like her should suffer all this unhappiness. She was aware that the Government intervened in matters relating to picking pockets, stealing and murder but drugs . . . why drugs? People bought drugs willingly and taking them made them feel better and revived their spirits. Safiyya decided that what people said on television about drugs was nothing but stupid exaggeration because even food could be very harmful if people did not control how much they ate. She was equally convinced that everything in the papers was a pack of lies because those who pontificate in them about drugs were the very same people who told lies about everything else in the country. As the circumstances of her life had become confused, perhaps she could not be blamed for consistently defending and glorifying evils of this kind. The feelings of injustice which she believed were inflicted by the Government were directed towards the Faculty of Law which she cursed vehemently, invoking God to curse it after each call to prayer, especially the dawn and the evening prayers, because she believed that her curses at these times would be more effective. Her favourite curse was "May a goddess destroy the Faculty of Law" because, in her opinion, it was from the Faculty of Law that the oppressive judge, who had passed the unjust and abominable sentence on her which decreed that she would be separated from her boys for twenty-five years, had graduated. For this reason she continued to hurl abuse in every possible direction, including the Leadership of the Republic and the Council of Ministers, on the basis that the sentence handed down under their law was inappropriate and unneccessary. These complaints were also one of the threads which tied Safiyya to Mahrousa because

Mahrousa, who was friendly with Safiyya's family, oversaw writing and sending the complaints for her. There was also a bond because of their close proximity in age and the common experience of bearing children but it was Safiyya's overwhelming generosity which was at the heart of the solid relationship between the two women. Safiyya gave generously to Mahrousa from gifts that her boys brought her on their visits to prison. This might be food, clothes and shoes – even medicines – which Safiyya shared with Mahrousa, especially medicines for rheumatism and colds. These were always in short supply at the pharmacies, especially during the winter months when there was a run on them, for reasons best known to the senior managers in the companies of the public sector. On top of this, Mahrousa considered Safiyya her private bank, often borrowing money from her from resources outside the prison. Inside prison the only currency which circulated was cigarettes. These were in such demand that you could get anything in exchange for them; the proportion of prisoners who smoked had reached at least ninety-nine per cent and the number of packets consumed depended on the individual prisoner's financial situation and the extent of her addiction. Naturally the amount consumed by those who were hooked on drugs, and by the prostitutes was more than the other prisoners. Mahrousa was in the habit of taking interest-free loans from Safiyya's sons when they came to visit their mother in prison or when she went to see them at home. No cloud hung over the relationship between the two "sisters"; Safiyya's husband even began to work in the video shop which Mahrousa's daughter, who now had a diploma in commerce, allowed him to run in return for a reasonable monthly income. He also became a conciliator in disputes which broke out over the car mechanic the girl wanted to marry. The mother flatly refused his proposal of marriage, swearing that none of her daughters would marry as long as she was alive. She considered men evil, created from the devil's rib, and her remaining daughters were in total agreement with this view perhaps because they were, both in looks and speech, exact replicas of their mother. The only exception was this youngest daughter, who had soft fair hair, made even finer by the force of gravity since it stretched down to the middle of her back. Her hair opened new prospects for her as regards men when the car mechanic, who had been bald since he was twenty-four, fell madly in love with her. She also used all kinds of beauty preparations on her face – red, blue and green – in order to stimulate his desire and encourage him to propose to her.

In deference to Safiyya's beloved husband who had intervened in this matter, Mahrousa finally agreed to the marriage after making over a large down payment for the bridal dower. She hoped that the marriage would end quickly and that her straying daughter would return to the pen, secure from Satan's rib and would rejoin her daughters' squad which was hostile to men.

For many years, Aziza watched the relationship between Mahrousa and Safiyya grow stronger and observed every minute aspect of the rope of love which stretched between them. As she spent long nights thinking about these women, she became obsessed with the desire to achieve justice and mercy on earth. She sipped her imaginary wine, inhaling deeply on the cigarettes which she smoked incessantly and which mingled with the smoke already in her chest. Her deep experience acquired in the women's prison had taught her that whenever she came across a true, caring relationship based on love and sincere devotion, like that which had sprung up and grown between Mahrousa and Safiyya, this kind of relationship was what really counted in deciding who to include amongst the passengers of the golden chariot ascending to heaven. She came to this conclusion despite the fact that she had never liked nor respected Safiyya because, as far as she was concerned, she was a tramp with a criminal nature and time had shown that, even if she were to live for a hundred years, she would be incapable of mending her ways. However, she would take her to heaven for the sake of Mahrousa, the warden with the angelic soul and devilish face who had shed so many tears of pain and torment and whose pure spirit and body was that of a true saint who could only be venerated in heaven. Aziza did not want to separate her from Safiyya's caring heart since she was the only person she had ever loved. She would give Safiyya one more chance and perhaps, if she ascended to this celestial world amongst angels which would be awaiting her and all the other women on the golden chariot, all the evil she had been tainted with in her earthly life would be erased. In any case, as her experience with Mahrousa had confirmed, she was not wholly devoid of good and her heart was not all black; there were some patches where light shone through which, given the chance, might spread and dispel all the darkness inside her. However, time was to extinguish any such hope. About two weeks after the day when Mahrousa's face was covered in honey, she found Safiyya lying in her bed one morning, in the final repose of death. Her glass eye stared ahead, in a way which made all the prisoners who had gathered around the motionless body, feel as if it was a real eye expressing sorrow and unhappiness as it fixed on the piece of blue sky which could be seen through the bars of the cell window nearby. Her expert hands, which had stolen for so long with ease and dexterity, now firmly gripped a photo of her two sons, resting on her chest. They smiled happily without fear for the future.

6

There Once Lived a Queen Called Zenobia

Doctor Bahiga Abdel Haqq had the rare distinction of being respected and liked by everyone in the prison, including the authorities. The latter were feared by most of the prisoners who submitted to their orders and avoided any contact with them unless absolutely necessary. This demarcation between ruler and ruled follows an old Egyptian tradition which history has taught us and which, time and again, has cost much blood and many lives. Beginning with the building of the pyramids, the tradition persisted throughout the period of anarchy which followed when the sixth dynasty and other later dynasties ruled and were periodically destroyed by the despotism of the Pharoahs. The latter's arbitrary system of rule, in which some were privileged at the expense of others, persisted during the period of the Persians, the Ptolemies, the Romans, the Arabs, the Mamluks, the Turks, the French and the British and re-emerged during the hunger riots in the winter of 1977. What history tells us is that any form of complaint and protest is bound to be suppressed and fail unless it has recourse to power and is able to challenge and undermine the ruling authority. This observation is borne out by the fate of those who failed to understand this lesson. It is personified by tragic heroes such as the Pharoe King and religious philosopher Akhenaten, or Hamam Al-Sohagi, whose dreams of national independence ended when a Mamluk military unit from Cairo descended on his house in the Saïd.

Bahiga Abdel Haqq did not command respect because she was a particularly nice, well-brought up young woman who belonged to the harmless world of innocence rather than to the world of deceit. Nor did she subscribe to the confrontational tactics which one encounters in every aspect of life. People respected her quite simply because she was a doctor. All doctors are revered the moment they join the Faculty of Medicine in a country where medicine is historically tied to wisdom, and where most of its inhabitants are poor peasants who elevate doctors to the ranks of the revered prophets, not because they relieve their tormented souls which rarely find any consolation, but because they relieve their bodies from the chronic pains and illnesses which they believe to be ordained by fate. As far as the prisoners were concerned, the crime Bahiga had been accused of was not dishonourable. If the authorities are to be believed, she caused the death of a young child, no more than nine years old, when she administered the wrong dose of anaesthetic during a tonsillitis operation in one of the private hospitals. Since the death of children in both urban and rural areas is a daily occurrence – like that of chickens – the prisoners believed that the matter should be kept in perspective instead of inflating it out of all proportion as the Government had done with Bahiga Abdel Haqq. It is also true that any woman who is blessed with being fertile can replace each child that dies, whether it be as a result of medical negligence during an operation or because of dehydration, stomach problems or diseases brought on by a lack of clean drinking water, traditional diets, bad health habits and the ineffectuality of the Ministry of Health in the provinces. Perhaps this ability to breed in large numbers explains why we have managed to survive as a people for seven thousand years and still do, despite the oppression and injustice we have suffered as well as all the occupations, plagues, the Nile droughts, the dehydration of children and the famines, on a par with the disasters suffered during Muntasir's reign.

The bitterness that Bahiga Abdel Haqq felt against humanity and the whole world was in no way alleviated by her short sentence of only three years. Nor was she consoled by the considerable respect she enjoyed in prison and the many favours she received from the prisoners in return for the health care and medical advice she gave them. She spent every moment of her life in prison consumed with hatred for life and was constantly contemplating suicide, although she never managed to go through with it. She resorted instead to biting her fingernails right down to the skin and their sorry, mangled state baffled anyone who saw them. She had the habit of fiddling nervously with strands of her hair, gazing with a sad, grave, defeated look in her eye. Her stomach kept a rare and involuntary pace with her agitated feelings, aggravated by the use of hydrochloric expectorant which allowed inflammation to settle in comfortably as well as an ulcer which was soon to take up residence in the lining of her stomach.

Bahiga was someone who demanded a great deal out of life but she gave lavishly in return. She was correct in her belief that the abilities she possessed earned her the right to a share of love from life which she never denied others. This basic equation was fundamental to the word 'justice', something Bahiga never stopped thinking about, despite her considerable intelligence. But she saw it as an elastic word which had lost its original, accessible meaning in law as defined by the legislator Hamurabi, who wrote "an eye for an eye, a tooth for a tooth". Now 'justice' had entered the celestial world of incomprehensibility. Perhaps this scepticism was partly behind the tragic aspect of Bahiga's personality. Ever since she could remember, she had strived to be a model of perfection because she believed that as such she could expect to receive her portion of justice and secure a favourable position in life. In order to achieve this she had to struggle in order to be different and transcend the constraints of her surroundings. Her first step in this direction was to seize the opportunity to attend school which her two elder sisters had been denied and so were permanently consigned to the bottom of the social ladder. She took maximum advantage of her amazing ability to understand and retain her lessons, despite the suffering she underwent in the depths of winter, clothed only in a thin linen uniform over a winceyette kaftan, handed down from one of her elder sisters, and despite suffering chronic hunger and near starvation because her father was so poor. Her meagre allowance of food was not sufficient to combat the dampness and cold which stopped the blood circulation in her limbs as she lay on a mat on the floor of her room to write her homework with a broken pencil. Nor was it enough to fight off the mild inflammation on her scalp caused by the kerosene her mother rubbed into it as a preventative against lice. Yet none of these disadvantages prevented Bahiga from coming first in her class from the time the magic world of learning first opened its doors to her. She was top in the first year and the second and third until she finished secondary school.

Bahiga was fortunate to go to school at the time she did. Ever since the age of the first Egyptian priesthood learning had been a privilege reserved for an élite minority which maintained its position in society in a number of ways, one of which was education. In this rare time of opportunity in our miserable history Bahiga, daughter of a nightwatchman, shared the same school seat with the daughter of a minister in the Government and both of them received the same dose of learning. But it is also true that the apparent justice associated with the policy of free education was a fallacy because the daughter of the nightwatchman could never, for a single day, be on a par with a minister's daughter when she was denied the same quality of food and did not sleep in a soft cosy bed. Neither was she lucky enough to have private lessons from the teachers at their school. However, thanks to competition, the daughter of Abdel Haqq, the nightwatchman, was able to make use of her ambition, her strenuous efforts and considerable intellectual abilities to get higher marks than any other secondary school pupil, including the minister's daughter. When Bahiga joined the Faculty of Medicine she entered a new and difficult stage in her struggle because, apart from her obvious motivation, she also concealed a burning ambition to fulfil her father's dream. Her father worked as a nightwatchman in one of the drug companies and, according to prevailing circumstances, he idealized doctors. He took up the hobby, albeit an enforced one, of giving injections in the muscle and vein to his sick neighbours who could not be moved to the clinics or were unable to get hold of night nurses. With the small sum he received in return, Abdel Haqq was able to go some way towards meeting the ever rising family expenses which arose from the failed economic policy of the state and the resulting inflation.

The nightwatchman's dream to see his intelligent daughter qualify as a doctor was never fulfilled because immediately after she obtained her secondary school diploma he died of cancer of the bladder, induced by chronic bilharzia. This made Bahiga even more determined to carry out her secret pledge to her father to be top of her year. Each year, on the anniversary of his death, she visited his grave with her mother and sister and would renew her pledge to him by reciting the opening verse of the Qur'an followed by the verse beginning "Say after me! There is only one God". As she placed green palm leaves and yellow daisies on his grave, she shed tears over his memory, promising him greater achievement in the coming academic year, despite the superhuman efforts she had already made, reminiscent of a soldier standing resolutely before the oncoming enemy, and despite the drain her studies had on the family's diminished resources. She was also faced with the problem of her inferior social status which became obvious when she was no longer able to conceal her poverty by wearing school uniform. There was no way she could keep pace with the girls and boys from the middle and upper classes who went around the campus, showing off the latest fashions. But despite all the psychological suffering this caused, she was able to hold her own by making herself simple clothes which were in good taste, taking ideas from some of the current magazines, especially *Eve*, the only women's magazine Bahiga could afford with the few piasters set aside from her meagre allowance. On one occasion she sent a letter to the magazine asking them how to get rid of the permanent dark circles under her eyes but she received no response because her letter went astray. Thus Bahiga continued to steer the ship of life against the strong waves and strove to fulfil the dream of her buried father.

If Bahiga was first in medicine, she was last in love. During the three years she spent at university she was approached by one of her fellow students whom she liked enough to agree to rendezvous outside the university campus. They would meet at the zoo or aquarium, along the banks of the Nile or anywhere else where they could snatch a few moments of love, which involved no more than the cost of a bus or train fare and the price of imported drinks like Coca Cola or Pepsi which they drank with *fuul* and *falafel* sandwiches. During that beautiful time Bahiga made a real effort to look as lovely as possible whenever she met her beloved, her husband-to-be. She tried a face mask made out of cornstarch and salt in an attempt to get rid of the pimples and to reduce the greasiness of her skin, and she spent an extremely restless night in hair rollers and pins to ensure that her hair would be beautiful for the following morning. At the time she believed she would fulfil her dreams; she only had two more years before graduating when she would undoubtedly be appointed one of the 'crew' of the teaching faculty. She was bound to graduate top, as usual, even though she had not benefited from the lessons which professors offered their rich students on the quiet in return for an exorbitant sum which their parents paid willingly from 'petrol cash', money plundered from the Government and the public sector, or from wheeler-dealing. Although she didn't anticipate a successful career for her beloved, since he had only scraped through his exams, she still considered him a suitable marriage partner, not least because he came from a slightly higher social class than she did. His father was one of the many officials in the government tax department whose salary barely met the needs of his large family while his mother helped make ends meet by contributing to the family income from the money she earned as a dressmaker. Financial circumstances dictated that Bahiga would have to gradually build the edifice of married life with her beloved, like a marital enclosure, joining their sticks together piece by piece, through the shared sweat and toil of their brows. More significantly, because he was a doctor like her, she would avoid the problems which might occur if she married a man who was less educated than her.

After two years, filled with hopes, dreams and burning passion, she discovered that she was clutching at straws. Her beloved husband, whom she considered vital to the imminent fulfilment of her dreams, let her down and found a new companion. He threw her over for another girl against whom Bahiga would fall at the first blow in the contest of female beauty whose father owned one of the famous shoes shops in the city and with whose money she rubbed the lamp of magic beauty. This enabled her to transform her coarse lack-lustre hair into strands of golden silk which framed a face covered in preparations by Max Factor, Helena Rubenstein, Yardley and Lancôme and others from the worldwide range of beauty manufacturers, no doubt contributing to their continued success. She had so much money that she could select a different outfit from her large wardrobe to wear each day she went to the faculty. More significantly, the girl who snatched away the joy of Bahiga's heart, granted him something that Bahiga never did because she wanted to preserve the proof of her virtue and modesty until the appointed hour, that of the wedding night. She also lost what she believed she clutched firmly in her left hand: she discovered that even though she had moved successfully through the primary, secondary stages and even through the years of her university studies, the priority of those about to embark on their careers was precisely calculated. Throughout Nasser's era, the tyrants of medicine had an old slogan beginning with three 'C's': a country estate, a car and a clinic, all of which were considered the ultimate aims of every successful doctor. Following the period of the open-door economic policy, this slogan was expanded to the point where they would own luxurious hospitals where any patient unable to afford to pay the exorbitant fees in advance would be left to die on the doorstep. These tyrants would never allow the likes of Bahiga Abdel Haqq, daughter of a nightwatchman in a drugs company, to participate in the holiest of holies and join the teaching faculty which had become a factory for shining stars of medicine, attracted to petro-money from Saudi Arabia and the Gulf, and commissions on deals. These same tyrants flew the extraordinarily gifted surgeon Magdi Yacoub to London, thus confirming the old saying: "There is no esteem for a prophet in his own country". They also unseated Bahiga from the throne of her dreams to face the bitter reality of our society. She was given only 'good' as a grade after they penalized her in the oral exams. She was in such a nervous state after losing her beloved that she could only stutter instead of answering their questions. Her confidence was not helped by the fact that her hair was scraped back in a bun and she was not looking well-groomed while the panel facing her wore suits and magnificent ties. The smoke from their pipes and foreign cigarettes mingled with the smell of well-known brands of after-shave, brought back from the capitals of the First World.

In this way Bahiga Abdel Haqq joined the thousands of doctors consigned to oblivion in the hospitals run by the Ministry of Health which, more than anyone, was in need of a cure for its chronic illness and inability to help a sick society which debilitated its people.

In the years that followed her graduation, Bahiga awakened to the reality of her humble status as a doctor which the state had valued at no more than one hundred and twenty Egyptian pounds. This barely covered the cost of one or two pieces of clothing necessary for work or four pairs of shoes which only lasted two or three months, possibly stretching to another month if she took them to be repaired instead of buying new ones. To be more precise, at that time her doctor's salary was no more than the price an upper middle class woman would pay to have her empty head tinted. This class was on the way to extinction in the shadow of new social changes in which learning was no longer valued. The West had smashed such aspirations after the fall of Nasser when the cherished memories of the Day of Celebration also fell from the collective consciousness. On this special day the brightest students in schools, institutes and universities had been honoured by Nasser, not only in his role as President of the Republic but also in his capacity as loyal leader who stood for the hopes of all the Arab peoples living between the Gulf of black oil and the Atlantic Ocean, where the poor of Morocco, a country squatting on the edge of the sea, are even deprived of the vegetation gathered from the forest to provide their basic subsistence.

Despite the years of hardship and toil, using her bare hands to move rocks which stood in her way, Bahiga could only mark time and was unable to move up the ladder. Her constant questioning of the reality of her existence and the absurdity of her social position finally drove her to a mild form of madness. She struggled with the conflict which arose from being respected but not valued. Naturally no one noticed Bahiga's mild schizophrenia because millions of other people suffered from the same complaint. She always dealt with patients and the medical team under her at work with the sobriety and earnestness required. Sometimes her manner was rather brusque: she would scold the nurses and was harsh with patients who didn't follow her instructions. But as soon as she left the hospital and went home, she would feel inadequate and inferior, particularly when she saw the smart cars racing through the streets of the city, driven by elegant, well-groomed women who looked like film stars. She felt worse when she window-shopped and saw that many of the goods she needed were so highly priced. As soon as she got home she would forget about the person she was at work and adapt completely to the humble shabby furnishings and the same simple food, served by her mother – a way of life which had hardly changed since she was a child.

The real cause of Bahiga's schizophrenia was the desire to find her place in the small pyramid she carried secretly inside her, just like everyone else, which acts as the gauge by which the individual defines his identity, seeking the esteem and respect of all those above him in the pyramid and scorning all those beneath him. The predilection that Egyptians have held since ancient times for these small, secret pyramids might explain why Egypt has the most complex and odious system of honorific terms and courtesy titles. The disparity inherent in her position in the pyramid caused Bahiga considerable confusion: she was one person during working hours and another for the rest of the day. Constant inflation and a low salary meant that her quality of life was hardly better than it was during the days she was struggling as a student. She eventually came to the conclusion that the question of marriage had become extremely problematic because despite the fact that she was quite presentable, if not exciting as far as men were concerned, it would be difficult to meet someone suitable as long as she worked for the Ministry of Health. In the government hospital, which was the extent of her social environment, she was surrounded by a number of men who were either already married because they were old or men whose ambitions revolved solely around their life in the Ministry. The cleverest doctors did not linger in the Ministry of Health but found alternative jobs in the private sector where they could earn a reasonable income, or to the public sector where they specialized, thereby increasing their opportunities. The young men on small salaries didn't even contemplate marriage, being content with fleeting emotional intrigues with the nurses in the hospital or with the type of women who understood the conditions of such games – a type Bahiga Abdel Haqq would never be.

Bahiga's problems were not helped by her family circumstances. Some of her elder brothers and her two elder sisters had not been educated. The result was predictable for the girls: one of them married a sewage worker and the other married with great difficulty because she was crippled by polio which she contracted before the government campaigns for inoculation had become widespread. The man married her because he was a widower with three children and worked part-time as a clerk filling in documents for illiterate people outside the courts. The brother, who was closest to her in age, finally obtained his secondary school certificate after failing repeatedly because he preferred to play 'sock ball' in the street instead of memorizing the reasons for the French campaign in Egypt. When he had reached these elevated heights, according to him at any rate, he volunteered for the army, escaping the unemployment that would certainly follow if he completed his education. Besides, he enjoyed the distinction of joining one of the professions which had authority. The other brother suffered from Down's Syndrome and lived until he was nineteen when God took him away, but he was only a minor consideration in the general problem of Bahiga's marriage which became more pronounced and complicated each day. Doctors, and those from the same social group who wanted to get married, did not consider Bahiga an attractive proposition. Rather the reverse because her lowly family background put them off; what, after all, was the attraction in a girl who had neither money nor beauty and whose family had no status? In one of his famous sayings the Prophet says: "Marry a woman for four reasons: for her money, her beauty, her pedigree and her piety; if you succeed with piety then your hands will be blessed." These were not times in which people were attracted by pious women unless they were from one of the Islamic fundamentalist organizations and Bahiga would never get a second look from a member of one of them because she didn't wear the veil. Nor was she excessively zealous in religious matters despite the fact that she always prayed and, during her years of studying, had always considered praying an important inspiration towards achieving her desired objective.

Some of Bahiga's relations and neighbours who were sympathetic to her predicament tried to provide her with suitors but the men who moved in their circles fell far short of her hopes and social ambitions. Some of them had only obtained the intermediary diploma and had lowly government jobs while others had very little education, despite a high income. One such hopeful suitor was a dealer in household appliances who had not progressed beyond the primary stage; he could hardly read and write, despite completing four years of school, which meant that when completing official documents, especially tax forms, he had to use a copper signet ring instead of signing his name.

On one occasion, Bahiga almost married the owner of a pharmacy in her quarter. His wife had recently died leaving him with four children, but she turned his proposal down when she discovered that his eldest child was almost the same age as her.

Bahiga then abandoned hope of ever getting married and pinned her hopes instead on working in one of the 'petrol countries' like so many did at that time. She saw this as a chance to realize her dream, still unfulfilled, to climb up the social ladder. She would then be able to attract men and have a wedding in which money was no object, an impossibility if she married one of her colleagues at the hospital who had limited means like herself.

However, instead of moving to a country with Volvos and Mercedes, where people travelled in aeroplanes to all corners of the world as if they were riding around in buses, Bahiga was moved to a place which she probably never thought existed on the map: this was the women's prison which was to house her in one of its cells.

Before this Bahiga was working in one of the small clinics which had sprung up, especially around the unplanned built-up areas on the outskirts of central Cairo and its old suburbs. They had spread like a cancer to accommodate the endless stream of migrants from the rural areas who came to the city in search of better living conditions. She started working there after the Ministry of Health instructed her to specialize as an anaesthetist. Her work at the clinic was over and above her regular morning work in the Ministry, and it earned her a modest income in return for performing the occasional minor operation when she was needed. The extra income enabled her to survive the month without continuing to borrow from her two sisters and their husbands, whom she would repay each month as soon as she received her salary.

However, unfortunately, she gave a fatal overdose of anaesthetic to a young child undergoing an operation. The parents of the dead child sued the owner of the clinic as well as Bahiga and both were found guilty of grievous bodily harm, causing the death of the child. Bahiga ended up with a three-year prison sentence while the doctor was fined several thousand pounds.

Bahiga spent many lonely, painful years in prison and was constantly dispirited by her inability to adapt to a world so totally alien to her and more dreadful than she could ever have imagined. When Bahiga was moved to a new ward she was introduced to "Madame Zaynab", the name all the prisoners, and even some of the warders, insisted on using for Zaynab Mansur. Zaynab Mansur was respected and was given special consideration by everyone in the prison, first and foremost because she was extremely beautiful. She had a low, gentle voice and languid eyes which people never tired of gazing at because they were so large and clear, the colour of pale almonds, and which harmonized with the colour of her white skin and her black hair, cut short to her neck, leaving a few wispy strands over her forehead and her ears. There was another reason behind the special treatment she received in prison and her immunity from the harassment other prisoners suffered from the prison authorities. Zaynab came from a well-established aristocratic family, some of whom held influential positions in the state machine. She was also a rich woman which made her popular with many of the prisoners who performed services for her like sweeping, polishing and cleaning the area allotted to her in the ward. They also washed her clothes and prepared food for her. Her unfailing humility and tolerance endeared her to everyone and her good sense made her particularly sought after as a mediator in disputes which broke out between the prisoners. She gave good advice and used her influential relations outside the prison to help solve some of the problems enountered by the prisoners inside.

Zaynab Mansur came to prison after killing her brother-in-law, her children's uncle. She murdered him with the ease and simplicity that could only be rivalled by a professional killer. People found it impossible to imagine that this beautiful, petite woman, as fragile as fine crystal, was capable of such a thing; they never knew how cool and collected Zaynab Mansur had been and that she could have done it a second, third or even a fourth time were she ever to be placed in a similar situation again.

Before this event Zaynab had led a charmed life full of joy and affection like the heroines in movies, with the exception of Egyptian movies naturally, as they would only make the comparison demeaning. Zaynab was the only daughter of a feudal lord of great standing, descended from a Mamluk family, mixed with Egyptian blood through the prestigious marriage of one of the male members of the family to the daughter of a Sheikh from al-Azhar, in the days when this great institution was both the religious and secular authority in the country. Her father lost his money after the 1952 Revolution when new agricultural reforms were introduced, dispossessing the large landowners. He then went into scrap metal until he became one of the biggest dealers in Egypt.

During this period Zaynab attracted a great deal of attention at social gatherings and in the noisy Cairo night clubs. She lead the way in fashion with magnificent clothes bought from the most famous Parisian designers, and which were more splendid than those of the models themselves. She created sensational stories about the passionate intrigues she was involved in which she circulated at evening gatherings, moving from one story to another with skill that could only be matched by Scheherezade herself when she narrated the *Thousand and One Nights*. The wretched youths at these gatherings did not usually feature in the stories themselves since they had no chance of ever getting near this alluring woman. Then just as iron can only be dented with iron, the beautiful Zaynab fell passionately in love with the handsome pilot of the plane flying her on one of her many trips to the West. He was an expert seducer of women, but never sought to enlarge his circle of victims because his job satisfied him and he had no desire to play the role of movie stars like Omar Sharif and Abdel Halim Hafez.

The handsome pilot was no less prosperous and noble than Zaynab, being descended from a family of Iranian origin which had settled in Cairo about two hundred years before and become famous carpet makers. After free secondary education was introduced, there was great competition to get into university and his mediocre results were not high enough to qualify him. He insisted on training as a pilot instead and joined a private flying school in which he soon gained promotion. Not long after his airborne meeting with Zaynab, he fathered two boys, both born by Caesarean. The law of genetics ensured that both boys turned out well: they inherited their mother's wonderful eyes, their father's long body and the best of their other features. However fate was to put an end to the young loving couple's chapter of happiness: Zaynab's husband was killed in a tragic air crash and a new chapter opened in Zaynab Mansur's life. Her husband had intended to give up flying and go into commerce instead so that he could be close to his family but the terrible accident wrecked their future plans. Not only was the life of this family turned upside down and the light extinguished in Zaynab's life but a strange and radical change took place in her personality which convinced everyone who knew her before that she had become a completely different woman. She lost her elegance, stopped wearing make-up and rarely went out, wearing the simplest of clothes which did nothing to show off her beauty. Then she reduced the times she mixed with people to the minimum and stopped the social activities she had pursued even after she married her pilot, now dead. In this way she became a model Egyptian widow and, except for rare occasions, she cut herself off like a hermit to bring up her children, smothering them with affection and care because they were now fatherless.

Zaynab was happy with her new existence in which her silent grief, which tormented her with beautiful memories of the past, became her constant companion. Her calm new life could have proceeded without disruption were it not for the only brother of her dead husband who had no intention of leaving Zaynab in peace to devote herself to the upbringing of her two boys. When he began to interfere in her affairs, it was not out of concern for the future happiness of his two nephews, but because he wanted to get hold of the considerable wealth they had inherited from their father. The latter had amassed his fortune from bringing back goods from all the corners of the world that his work had taken him. There was tight control over such imports from the West under Nasser's stringent economic policy so they were sold illegally in small shops, scattered in the high-class suburbs of the city, by small traders who made large profits. This illicit trade formed the base of a much wider trade boom when restrictions with the West were lifted under Sadat.

Each time the uncle tried to impose his unofficial guardianship on the small family Zaynab lay in ambush, ready to foil his plans. She refused all his offers to invest the boys' money, as well as his plans to buy real estate and apartments to let out furnished because she was always suspicious of his intentions and felt that he would get her into trouble. When these plans failed he tried to win her affection, and even proposed to her. She naturally refused and was genuinely astonished at the audacity of this latest move since he was well aware of the enormous place her husband occupied in her heart. She never imagined he was the kind of person who would devalue such sentiments of love and affection. When he failed to gain custody of the two boys by using tactics as crafty as Dimna and Baydaba the philosopher, characters known for their cunning from a famous book of Arabic fables, he was consumed with hatred for his sister-in-law and turned his mind to finding some legal means of achieving his aim. He had been humiliated when she turned down his proposal, telling him that a thousand men couldn't take the place of her beloved husband. He began to spread rumours about her, attacking her reputation and honour, but this didn't bother her because she knew that in time people would realize they were unsubstantiated; she brought some of her relatives round to her side who threatened to cut off his tongue unless he stopped spreading these rumours immediately. Then a hellish idea took root in his mind while he was watching an Egyptian film by Yahya Shahin, who borrowed the plot from Charlotte Bronte's novel, *Wuthering Heights*. He would outmanoeuvre his brother's widow and put himself forward as legal guardian to the two boys instead of her parents who were both dead.

Ever since she was small, Zaynab Mansur had been crazy about cats, perhaps because it was also her mother's passion. Zaynab grew up in her father's large house in Munira which, at the time, was one of the most beautiful, select districts of Cairo. It was not unusual to find her mother lavishing the same affection on a cat or two that she would give to a child. She would often lie on her bed, reading a paper or magazine, with a great big cat perched on her chest, purring happily against her face. Perhaps this is how Zaynab became fond of these beautiful vain creatures which always manage to gain the upper hand over their master or mistress, making them pander to their every whim. For whatever reason, the young Zaynab still had lots of cats when she was living in her father's house before she married, and a young maid from amongst the retinue of servants was instructed by her wealthy father to devote herself exclusively to looking after the cats.

After Zaynab married she virtually abandoned this hobby because, as a young wife madly in love, she wanted to devote herself wholeheartedly to her husband – with the exception of one black Persian cat with long fur. As soon as her sons were born, the whole idea of cats went right out of her mind.

When her husband died and the two boys were over infancy, Zaynab was left feeling bored in the large, two-storied house in Masr Jadida. At this point she resumed her old hobby of raising cats, helped by the boys who were just as keen. The house was soon inhabited by fifteen living creatures, which apart from the family included a dozen cats of different shapes, colours and sizes. Each one had its own name and particular place to sleep in and they led a wholesome, healthy life as well as being pampered with silk or velvet ribbons and bells. Zaynab bought beautiful pieces of cloth to make coats for the cats in anticipation of the cold winter days and nights and designed them to allow freedom of movement for their supple bodies. This necessitated an additional outlay over and above what was spent on their food and little toys and the cats were in a state of perpetual joy and excitement. Although the money spent on the cats was minimal in proportion to the income of this wealthy family, when viewed through the critical eyes of the uncle, who was spying on every detail of his dead brother's family, this way of carrying on was nothing short of lunacy.

Zaynab then developed an enthusiasm for *zar* ceremonies which the uncle, who was extremely practically minded and kept any kind of involvement with spirituality to a minimum, considered abnormal behaviour. These ceremonies she attended were a vociferous form of ritual occasion, a new craze that spread like a disease amongst working class women and spread to the upper classes after the fad of loose fitting *gallabiyas* and wooden clogs and the mass viewing of tawdry sex films disappeared following the disaster of the 1967 war. Zaynab not only participated in the *zar* ceremonies but allowed them to take place in her large house, throwing herself into the frenzied dancing and gyrating her body which had given up any other kind of activity. Apart from one or two men playing African-style instruments which beat out the popular rhythm this kind of ritual was usually reserved for women. The male instrumentalists were normally regarded to be above suspicion as far as sexual virtue or modesty were concerned but the uncle objected to these rituals which went on late into the night. A great deal of money would be spent on one party – as much as on a dozen cats – in order to supply the necessary, sometimes impossible, conditions, imposed by the experts organizing these ceremonies and those supervising its rituals. They might demand a pair of goats which had to be pure white except for a black blaze on the head or a brown spot on the tail; sometimes they required birds and animals which were difficult to get hold of in a country which is situated on the Tropic of Cancer and not on the Equator. One time they asked the widow to bring an Indian parrot with red and yellow feathers and place its cage on the window ledge in the room where the *zar* would take place. It could then join in with a running commentary all night, repeating sections of the frenzied, magical songs being chanted. Zaynab paid an exorbitant price for the parrot which she bought from the zoo at Giza after asking one of her relations, appointed as a senior director of this zoo a year before, to intercede on her behalf.

In a session held to discuss the uncle's request for custody, the court was not convinced by his point of view, nor by the evidence put across by his shrewd lawyer, who tried with all means possible to prove the mother's madness. The judge turned down his offer to present a video of her dancing, which showed her reeling like a drunkard in one of the *zar* ceremonies; he had been invited to a formal lunch by one of the most eminent doctors in the city and wanted to finish quickly because he felt hunger pangs in his stomach. The judges were also of the opinion that the uncle had a weak case and rejected his evidence. Zaynab's attitude to cats and the *zar* ceremonies was not so extraordinary as to merit being called abnormal in a society where superstitions abounded; many people kept to their traditional beliefs which went back even further than primitive Africa and the Middle Ages to several thousand years before Christ. Then the widow's lawyer, who was no less smart than the litigant's lawyer, managed to sway the judges in her favour after he persuaded the court that her interest in pets was a phenomenon of modern civilization and progress. He supported his argument with several cuttings he had taken from local and foreign newspapers about people who were so fond of pets that they had bequeathed all their wealth to their favourite cat or dog. He stated how in Paris, the capital of culture and enlightenment, he had witnessed with his own eyes – and here it must be said that he was lying – immaculate rubbish collectors assigned to clear dog faeces left on the streets while the children in the poor quarters of the city evacuated their bowels against the walls and under the windows without anyone noticing. Then he turned to the question of *zar* ceremonies and commended them as a means of psychological therapy which had been developed through the ingenuity of the people. They had discovered the important role the *zar* played in releasing their mental and physical frustrations before having access to the specialized methods for dealing with such problems, developed through academic research. He underlined the necessity to take all branches of traditional medicine seriously in order to confront the fierce imperialist invasion which had come to a head in the defeat of 1967 and which not only targeted the freedom and resources of the country but also its culture and heritage. The court listened to his extended rhetorical speech which Zaynab noticed was full of exaggeration and repetition, darting from one thing to another and mixing everything up. Then the judge gave a surprise decision: in the first part of his verdict he overturned the charge of insanity, but it didn't console Zaynab as it might have done because he went on to grant custody of the boys to their uncle. The judge decided that even if her mental faculties were in good order, as confirmed by the medical report in her file, she was undoubtedly a spendthrift who was not to be trusted with her sons' assets, cash and investments and given that the uncle was a businessman he was better qualified to have custody. The uncle had convinced the judge of his business acumen by securing, through an intermediary, the short term contract for a flat in a splendid apartment block in Nasr city.

Shortly after the verdict, Zaynab Mansur stood at the door of the courtroom, looking at the new guardian of her children with complete calm and composure. He left the chamber where the verdict had just been read and appeared at the door at which point Zaynab took out her husband's licensed gun, which she had loaded the night before with three bullets, and aimed it at the uncle's chest. His mocking, vengeful smile suddenly became contorted into an expression of intense pain which made him grit his teeth. Zaynab felt her spirits lift after the long period of psychological trauma she had suffered since the uncle first took legal proceedings against her. She had even felt relief when the verdict went against her because the action she was about to take would place her in the position of victor rather than vanquished. She had never, for a single day, been one to submit in the way someone delicate and pampered might do, but always triumphed at whatever cost, as princess of her own destiny, making her own life choices just as Zenobia Palmeira did in ancient times.

Thanks to the lawyer's commendable judicial efforts and her powers of influence, Zaynab was sentenced to only seven years. She was extremely grateful to get off so lightly.

Zaynab entrusted everything concerning money and property to her cousin on her maternal side who was like a sister to her and a second mother to her two boys. The boys also inherited the murdered uncle's estate because he had never married and had no other heirs.

In prison, Zaynab found the young doctor, Bahiga, very charming and from the time she first joined the ward she had a great deal of respect for her. After a while, Zaynab discovered that Bahiga fulfilled a long-held wish in the world of friendship, not only inside prison but in the world outside as well. Zaynab had never experienced the happiness which can come from true friendship between two women, because throughout her life men had stood in the way. Being beautiful, she was solely preoccupied with the interest they showed in her and in how she was always the object of their gaze and admiration. Of course she knew many women but she never got to know a woman intimately in the way that she knew Bahiga Abdel Haqq in prison. From the time they first struck up a friendship together and began to share many aspects of their daily lives, Bahiga became a substitute for the family Zaynab had lost, and Zaynab became the sole source of comfort in Bahiga's desolate life. Bahiga had never experienced the intimacy she shared with Zaynab and had never felt able to confide her innermost anxieties and pain to any woman before. Bahiga dazzled Zaynab with her skill in performing amazing tricks with paper, making birds, pitchers and exquisite brides out of paper remnants which she came across by chance in prison. There were also other entertaining tricks which she did with matchsticks and small pieces of macaroni and Zaynab joined in these games which were like mathematical problems and complicated riddles. Zaynab did Bahiga a great favour by teaching her French which she had never learned because she was part of a generation which, not unnaturally, scorned foreign languages as a reaction to long years of British colonialism and European monopoly over the country. This generation, which was influenced by nationalist feelings and exalted their own language above any other, is the same generation which demonstrated how the memory of nations can fade in certain eras. It quickly threw its own children into the bosom of foreign education, in the hope that they would catch the train of civilization which they had missed and in so doing neglected Arabic, the mistress of all languages, forgetting the fact that even though the Indians master the English language better than the Japanese, it is the Japanese who are economically more advanced.

It was Bahiga who introduced Aziza to Zaynab and related her story after a strong relationship had built up between them. Aziza valued Bahiga's excellent advice about her severe and painful haemorrhoids. Her inactive life and the lack of any suitable food containing roughage were not conducive to regular motions so that her condition had become chronic. Aziza, through her slightly mad perspective, credited Bahiga with many qualities: her education, her refinement, her straightforward way of dealing with any situation which differed from the deceitful tactics employed by all the other women she knew. She behaved in a dignified, straight manner without being self-indulgent and trivial. For that reason, while her gaze wandered into the distance on a clear moonlit night to rest on the wispy outline of the tall trees which she could see from her cell window, she decided to include Bahiga and her friend Zaynab in the golden chariot with the winged horses, ascending to heaven. The overriding factors which influenced her decision were first that she would undoubtedly need a skilful doctor like Bahiga to cope with any problem which might arise with the passengers selected for the journey; second she would need a sensitive, refined woman like Zaynab to teach the other wretched women the elements of good manners and etiquette because she had long disapproved of the coarse behaviour and obscene speech which most of the prisoners adopted amongst themselves. For those reasons, and while she was sitting sipping her water as if it were wine, savouring the last puff of her cigarette, she gazed at the wisps of the tree again and said, "I have good news for you Bahiga. Tomorrow when you come up with us I have a well-equipped clinic for you with everything you need." Then she added:

"And you, Madame Zaynab, make sure you pack the clothes before we take off."

7

Grief of the Sparrows

This creature, as white as a turnip heart, who was so thin that half of her seemed to be missing, was the bewildered young girl known by everyone in the women's prison as "Silent Shafiqa". Her origins and the sequence of events which brought her to the women's prison were a complete mystery to everyone. Neither did anyone know who her parents were, nor the name they had originally given her.

One day she arrived at the prison on a charge of begging and thereafter returned to the prison repeatedly on the same charge, as one of its many short-term prisoners. Anyone with the slightest intelligence would have noticed Shafiqa's confused state of mind, except for the doctors, that is, who insisted that she was was perfectly sane, thus denying her the honour of entering the state psychiatric hospital. This institution, which had long been one of the landmarks in the country, was a stopping place for those who couldn't bear the inconsistencies and futility of life, but to enter that institution was merely to jump out of the frying pan into the fire. Perhaps the psychiatrists were justified in their assessment of Shafiqa, since she was an extremely calm person who never quarelled and would never harm a living creature, not even a little ant which could be crushed under her feet as it crossed her path. Above all she was always smiling. It is true to say that she never spoke and never replied to any question put to her, but isn't silence in a world raging with nonsense a sign of ultimate sanity rather than madness?

It was quite normal for everyone to find acceptance in the women's prison, especially a case like Shafiqa who caused few problems apart from the concern and anguish she aroused in others. The other prisoners, who were bewildered by her and sympathetic towards her condition, felt frustrated by their failed attempts to rehabilitate her by getting her to eat and dress normally. She rarely had a bath or took off her shift which she always wore close to her skin, with nothing under or over it. She never asked or shouted out for food, whether it was for bread or for something which was rare in prison like meat, and if one of the prisoners didn't take it upon herself to fetch her something to eat or drink, she would remain for long periods, sometimes days, eating hardly anything at all. She was often seen throwing her daily ration, which was three flat loaves of stale, brown bread, to the stray cats in the prison courtyard or breaking the bread into crumbs which she left on the window ledge of the cell for the little birds which occasionally flew in from the trees close to the prison.

Sometimes Silent Shafiqa would be seen bending over on the prayer rug on the floor for long periods, as if she was doing yoga, while at other times she could be seen lifting her frail little hand with its thin worm-like fingers to face the rays of the sun so that she could examine the intersecting lines of her palm. This would go on for long periods without her showing any sign of restlessness; she seemed more like a statue carved out of rock and for that reason she was named "Silent" and lived amongst the other prisoners without quarrelling with them or showing any trace of malice towards them.

Despite Shafiqa's state of mind she was perfectly aware of what had happened to her and still suffered from the terrible torment which had made her mute. She chose to cut herself off from the world and renounce communication with other people, despite all attempts to encourage her to talk. The psychiatrists and neurologists, the ear, nose and throat specialists and the speech therapists had all confirmed that her vocal apparatus and hearing mechanisms were in good order and that there was no reason why she should not speak. When they eventually gave up they were inclined to think that her inability to speak was the result of some trauma she had suffered and the story behind her condition remained a secret to all except her. Only she lived through its every detail, moment by moment, suffering unimagined torment. Perhaps this was behind her enigmatic smile, which mystified everyone, and broke from her thin, tightly-closed lips when a deaf and dumb specialist was brought to try and get through to her during the court investigation, in order to take her statement in the official hearing. It may also have influenced their decision to convict her since this smile, which appeared every time the expert did sign language in an attempt to communicate with her, was tinged with scorn, not for the abortive attempt to reintegrate her into the world but for all the falsehood and evil around her which she discovered through her suffering and which made her resolve never to communicate with others, however much they tried and however important it might be for her.

The strange thing was that Shafiqa had never, for a single day, been a beggar. She never begged from anyone and never walked the streets with her hand outstretched, asking favours from people, be it money or something to eat or drink. She would simply sit against the wall of the mosque, sleep under a tree in one of the public gardens or walk along the edge of the river until her bare feet were so tired that she would crouch down on the pavement, resting her hands in her lap, completely sapped of strength.

On such occasions, her pitiful appearance would move the hearts of passers-by, some of whom threw her a few coins or a piece of the semolina cake that lovers eat as they walk along the river bank at sunset. Even though she made no use of the money, except to slip it into a bag made from paper discarded in the street, the officer who led her to the police station considered the paper bag of money evidence that she was a professional beggar who exploited people's sympathy and this was duly recorded at the investigation.

The profound grief which Shafiqa continued to suffer was the sum of all that she felt in life and was evident to anyone who had eyes by simply looking at her face. To look at her was to sense the tears flowing continually from her widely-set eyes with their noble, mournful expression, although these tears were never visible. Perhaps this look explained the gentle treatment she received instead of the coarseness, violence and attempted assault which someone in her position could usually expect – the verbal assaults of mockery and rude words or bodily assaults to which a young girl without any protection is exposed. She was probably also saved by her filthy appearance and the fact that she had often spent her nights in dark, deserted places or amongst ruins, all of which added to her estrangement.

Before her life of vagrancy and solitude, Shafiqa had lived like any ordinary lower middle class girl from a peaceful home. Deprived of their mother, the family was cared for by her widowed sister who was about eight years older than her. She carried out her role as caring mother efficiently and was also an affectionate sister to Shafiqa and her two brothers, one of whom was older and the other who was four years younger. This arrangement meant that their father, who valued the unity of his family and its continued success, decided against marrying again after his wife died, despite his worries and the constant loneliness which made him anxious and nervous. He would lose his temper for the slightest reason and was extremely strict with his family, especially the daughters, for fear that they would run wild without a mother to watch over them. As a true man from the Saïd, who upheld values and traditions stretching back several thousand years, he was determined to preserve the reputation of his family which he placed above any other consideration in life.

Shafiqa's widowed sister was very feminine and beautiful. Her features bore clear Circassian traces, a testimony to the fact that the Ottoman authorities of the Sublime Porte had once passed through. These features had attracted proposals of marriage since the time she was fifteen, eventually leading there when she was seventeen. Her husband was a prosperous army officer who left home early one Thursday morning in 1967, never to return, leaving her with three children, the youngest of whom was still sucking at her breast. He was recognized as a martyr and the grieving widow was accordingly entitled to all the distinctions due to the families of martyrs.

The *fatwa* issued on her husband's death, officially recognized this beautiful woman as a widow in the state records, a status she maintained until the last moment Silent Shafiqa saw her. After her husband disappeared and she lost all hope of his ever returning, she resolved to never repeat the experience and lived for many years without any desire to enter into family life with another man. However, the laws of nature, which are well known, brought her into the arena once more but with one fundamental difference: the new experience was an affair of passion which could never develop into marriage because of the different religious backgrounds of the two lovers. This forced her to shroud their relationship in total secrecy for fear that her father and the rest of her family, particularly her brothers, would discover the affair. This fastidious and conscientious sister, who also worked as a teacher, always used the private lessons she gave to young male and female students as a pretext to meet with her lover out of official working hours. When she returned she would hasten to conceal any trace which might disclose her relationship with him, like the little presents he gave her from time to time. These were nothing more than bracelets or silver rings or a bottle of perfume called 'Destiny' which was locally made. The imported perfumes were not well-known at the time due to the economic boycott of the West which had been applied more stringently since the defeat of 5th June but ended like a storm in a tea cup by the mere implementation of Sadat's new economic policy. She had recently begun to offer these simple gifts to her younger sister as a token of her love and esteem and the strong attachment she felt towards her. Shafiqa was increasingly influenced by her sister and behind the esteem and admiration she felt for her was the surrogate role of mother she performed in absence of the real mother whose womb she came from. But her beauty and her striking femininity made Shafiqa feel she was a young girl lacking in femininity, whose beauty had already faded, and she dreamed of being like her elder sister who was everything that was marvellous and honourable. This widow and lover remained faithful to her love, which became more inflamed with each day that passed, because of her lover's oath of eternal devotion. He vowed that he would never end the relationship, whatever happened and whatever the pressure from his old mother who arrived every day, crying and kissing his hand, beseeching him to marry as soon as possible because, according to family tradition, his younger brother would never be able to marry unless his elder brother married first. In the zoological garden under a huge tree, which might have been planted as far back as the time of Khedive Ismail, the two lovers swore to be faithful. They carved out the first letters of their two names with a nail file, sealing their secret in a frame which, far from the Pharaonic, was in the shape of a heart, pierced by an arrow. They swore that only death, which destroys sensual pleasure and separates people – as Scheherezade said in the *Thousand and One Nights* – could stand between them and disrupt the communion of love which extended between their two hearts.

The unfortunate lover, who suppressed her feelings and anxieties over a long period, fearing discovery of her affair, was under terrible strain because she was beautiful and attractive to men. She turned down many marriage proposals from suitors prepared to take on her children. When she refused, she always adhered firmly to the excuse that she would never relinquish the upbringing of her children to anyone and would continue to care for her father and brothers and sisters. In an attempt to conceal some of her beautiful features and to avoid attracting attention, she wore a veil which covered the lovely coal-black hair adorning her head and her white face, with its perfectly proportioned features. In this way she hoped to give the impression that she was virtuous, just as any young widow from a conservative Saïdi family who is mindful of her martyred husband's reputation and faithful to her sons might do. However, one day, despite all her efforts, her affair became public knowledge when one of her relations put two and two together. He had been passionately in love with her for a long time, going back to the days before her marriage. At that time he hadn't dared ask for her hand because he owned a small shop, selling cigarettes, candy and Needlers multi-flavoured boiled sweets which were cheap and popular with several generations of children before the appearance of Chicaboom, Chiclets and other products from the Sima sweet factory. But the flourishing tourist industry improved his circumstances greatly, especially after he converted his shop into a tourist restaurant for fast food, removing its familiar emblem – a kerosene lamp with the number five placed on the glass counter to illuminate the cigarettes on sale. A partner provided the capital for the restaurant which was called 'The Well-Garnished Table'. His partner had earned several thousand dollars after years of working on an oil station in Saudi Arabia and the shopkeeper's improved financial status reawakened the amorous feelings which had remained dormant during all the years his loved one had been married and borne three children. For these reasons he made her an offer of marriage on terms which were extremely advantageous, considering the lack of activity in the marriage market at the time. But the bewildered widow rejected the tempting proposal using the same pretext which earned her the increasing respect of her father and brothers – feigning eternal fidelity to her dead husband. She maintained she had a symbolic role to keep the memory of her deceased husband alive and wished to sacrifice herself entirely to the welfare and happiness of her children.

The shopkeeper, who had begun to call himself a business man since transforming his shop into a restaurant, was able to dabble in other investments because of the profit he made from selling cheap traditional food which the tourists and the foreigners found distinctively eastern. But he still clung to the hope that he might win over the woman he had desired for so long. Indeed his desire had become even more ardent since she had matured, like a tasty fruit ready to be plucked. His determination to marry her was also an attempt to restore his peace of mind and regain confidence the lack of which had discouraged him from proposing when he owned the confectionery shop. But the strongest factor behind his determination was his increasing conviction, formed since entering the jungle of business, that money could buy everything. Indeed he considered money the only source of a meaningful existence in life. Thus the man of business tried every means possible to approach the widow who was passionately in love with someone else. Unable to give her presents directly since she would merely have refused them, he successfully ingratiated himself with her sons and family by giving them presents instead. He also did them favours which, for a family in their circumstances, would have been difficult to obtain elsewhere. He found her eldest brother a job in a tourist agency and presented her father with a hearing aid imported from Switzerland. This was to relieve him from the voices which echoed constantly in his right ear, like the sound coming from the bottom of a deep well. But despite all these attempts the wife he aspired to not only sent him packing without hope but she did it with tight-lipped contempt and a look of utter disdain. It was absolutely unthinkable that someone who was growing balder by the day, with a paunch that swelled as he grew more prosperous, could ever have the same place in her heart as the lover whose face was beautiful enough to be one of the famous Fayoum icons. She was justified in believing that this business man would only treat her sons well and be affectionate with them at the time of his proposal and that his behaviour towards them would change after they were married.

As a merchant, who had a wide experience of life and of dealing with many different types of people, men and women, the persistent suitor guessed there was something mysterious about the whole affair – that there must be another man involved – since it was inconceivable that a woman, like this beautiful widow, would not want a relationship with someone of the male sex. This was confirmed by the small details which gave her away, despite all her attempts to conceal her desire. She would watch the television soaps and sentimental films with passionate intensity; sometimes he would interrupt one of these sessions by making a surprise visit to her home and she would delay going to prepare tea or coffee for him because she was loath to miss any of the serial. He also noticed that even though she wore a veil, she put on make up and perfume when she went out to give her private lessons. She was also extremely punctual with her appointments, like a soldier going to join his military unit. He tried to entice her away from the numerous private lessons she gave by offering her a new pupil, the son of a wealthy Arab, who would pay twice what she earned for just one lesson a week in addition to chauffeur-driven transport in a limousine. But she absolutely refused, using the pretext that she was frightened of going to the homes of Arabs from the Gulf, even if the wife and children were there, because she was mindful of her reputation.

After that he was left with no alternative but to search for the reason behind her decision to refuse him, despite his wealth which was enough to attract a young virgin like the shining moon, in the bloom of youth and ripeness, or a spinster who dreamed of marriage let alone a widow with three children. And this reluctant lover realized full well that he was right in thinking he could have all the young and beautiful women he wanted because most young men were unable to marry and shoulder the cost of furnishing the marital home. The era of middle men had destroyed all possibility of realizing the dreams and ambitions of a better life through job opportunities: from the needle to the spaceship the slogan "industrialize!" had crashed. Without paying anything he could also have married a signora of his choice from amongst the foreign girls blown into his restaurant by the winds of tourism. He decided to spy on the widow's movements when she was out, especially in the afternoons when she went off to give her private lessons. He would sometimes come to visit a short while before the time of her class on the pretext that he had some work to see to in their house. He then insisted on giving her a lift in his private car to her supposed lesson in order to follow her afterwards. Naturally it didn't take long before he discovered her secret lover; he followed her to her rendezvous in one of those dimly lit, discreet places usually frequented by lovers who prefer to conduct their passionate exchanges in such romantic settings and where the waiters whisper as they serve their whispering customers.

Unfortunately Shafiqa's sister didn't notice the intruder who took a good look at her and perhaps the matter would have ended there if only she could have brought herself to accept his proposal. She knew perfectly well that should her father ever discover her affair, she would die. But because she did not see him she unwittingly sealed her own miserable fate when the business man carried out a shameless act of revenge. He weighed up the pros and cons and came to the conclusion that she would continue to reject his proposal because of the other man, who in his view was a pig who had obstructed him, inflicting a terrible wound to his pride, now scarred for life. Thus he took it upon himself to inform the father that he had seen her sitting with a strange man in Abu Manjal's, a coffee house of ill repute, mainly known as a retreat for lovers. She was seen sitting with her legs crossed, hand in hand with the man who had his other arm around her, whispering words full of love and passion.

When the father learned of his daughter's behaviour, he considered it the height of shame and depravity and unthinkable for a woman who had been given the best possible conservative upbringing according to the tradition of the Saïd. To make matters worse, and as her brother confirmed through his own investigations, the man she was seen with was from a different religion. On a cold winter's night following this revelation, the austere old man calmly took his momentous decision. He consulted first with his son who was no less angry and took a similar hard line towards the behaviour of his widowed sister who, in his view, had sullied the family's honour. One day after sunset, the brother tricked his sister into accompanying him on one of the shopping expeditions they often went on together, suggesting they should go and choose him a shirt and some socks. After she had quietened her three young children, who were screaming because they wanted to go with her, and had promised to bring them back a carton of their favourite fruit juice, she kissed them goodbye and her brother whisked her off in his car. This was the same sister who had so often held him by the hand after her mother died, washed his clothes for him and had even suckled him at her little breast devoid of any milk. She attempted to give him the security of his mother's breast which he had been denied during the critical nights immediately following her death – nights in which the silence was broken by the baby's heart-rending screams for his mother's milk. The brother did not take her as expected to Umr Effendi's shops, recently renovated to suit the mood of the times, and which had started selling the most magnificent shirts instead of the cheaper clothes made from winceyette, coarse cotton and poplin. Instead he took her to her destined fate in an area of remote desert, a few kilometres from the city and its suburbs. Waiting for her there, under the cover of darkness, was a hired assassin with whom the father had previously made an agreement. Her brother cruelly dismissed all her entreaties and pleas to spare her for the sake of her little children who at that moment were longing for the cartons of juice she had promised to bring them when she returned.

The son returned to the solemn house and with a heart as hard as stone and a cold and deathly look in his eyes, like that of the assassin himself, he announced the successful completion of his mission to his father who was sitting, waiting impatiently for news of the outcome of his plan. He was reassured that he had been cleansed of his shame as soon as the announcement, which soothed his heart, had been delivered. He called the younger sister, who was none other than Silent Shafiqa and told her, as he lay stretched out on his bed, what had happened to her sister, the children's mother, threatening her on pain of death if she so much as breathed a single word on the matter to anyone.

That night Shafiqa, whose name up to that moment was Taghrid, lay stretched out on her bed like a stiff corpse waiting to be washed, eyes wide open, weakened by the mad burning force which rose from within her and incapable of making the smallest movement, even closing her eyelids. By the time the sun rose, she had lost eight kilos in weight as if she were a small piece of butter which had melted one hot night. When the children of her deceived sister woke up to find their mother was not by their side at home, they began to cry bitterly. She could not think what to say to them except that their mother had gone to stay with her aged paternal aunt who was very ill. But as evening set in, the suddenly bereaved young girl was totally unable to face up to the situation and was transformed into an oddity only a metre and a half tall and weighing just forty-five kilos. At around midnight, when she was sure that everyone was asleep, including her father and brother, the wretched young girl tiptoed out to the front door of the apartment and opened it cautiously and quietly. Her father was snoring and only discovered her escape when he was awakened later by the sound of a metal saucepan lid falling on the floor. A stray cat had knocked over the saucepan while trying to remove its lid.

The girl, who from this moment became known as Silent Shafiqa, ran and ran as if propelled by the headstrong will of a young filly. Finally, running on and on in an attempt to erase the image haunting her mind, she collapsed against a wall, exhausted. It was one of the high brick walls outside schools, a relic from the time of the colonial missionaries in the last century. She remained in this position until just before daybreak when she was noticed by someone on his way to seek additional blessing from God at the morning prayer in the mosque, close to the school. As soon as he caught sight of her he begged God's protection from the Devil because in all the sixty years of his life, he had never witnessed a human being so thin and with such eyes, staring blankly into the distance, at this time of the night when most people were asleep. When he returned with some fellow worshippers immediately after the end of the prayers to show them the sight he had just witnessed, the terrifying creature had fled. He was mocked by his companions who told him that what he had seen must have been a figment of his imagination.

From the time she spent her last night in her father's house, Shafiqa never uttered another word. Day and night she wandered aimlessly about, scrounging from rubbish dumps and sleeping against any wall she could find, even if it was a graveyard wall. She spent most of her time on the move in an attempt to avoid attracting people's attention, never returning to the same place, cutting through the streets and alleyways from one end of the city to the other. Only a few months had passed before her features were transformed into those of another, bearing no resemblance whatever to her old self. After she was told about her sister's murder, her hair had turned white overnight and she took on the appearance of someone at least twenty-five years older than she really was.

A few months later, Shafiqa was convicted for begging, a sentence she was to receive repeatedly in the future until she became one of the permanent inmates of the prison.

Aziza only decided to include Silent Shafiqa amongst the troop of women going on the golden chariot to heaven because she felt so sorry for her. She was moved by the terrible degree of wretchedness and pain which was evident from her appearance as well as her austere demeanour, denying herself, in the way that the Sufi mystics do, all earthly things which people usually covet in life. Aziza was particularly attracted by the tenderness she showed towards the little sparrows and the gentle way she fed them by placing bits of bread for them on the window ledge. If Aziza had known Shafiqa's story she would have placed her directly and without any doubt or hesitation at the top of the list of passengers in the chariot. And for the sake of Shafiqa, Aziza decided to include Hajja Umm Abdel Aziz in the chariot, not because Aziza felt Umm Abdel Aziz was pitiable and did not deserve to be imprisoned nor because she was one of the victims of life whom fate had tossed into this dreadful place, just as the waves of the sea toss the corpses of the drowned onto the deserted shores. Aziza was neither swayed by the prayer rituals she performed day and night and her incessant reading of righteous verses nor, for that matter, by the long periods she spent tuned into the station which broadcasts the Glorious Qur'an on a small transistor radio stuck close to her ear. This radio was made by Telemasr, a testimony to Egypt's failed attempt to enter the field of manufacturing and become self-reliant in the days when there was tumultuous propaganda about the rocket known as Qahir and its brother Zafir, both of which failed to secure any kind of victory in the 1967 war. The reason Aziza decided to admit her to the chariot was because of the compassion she constantly and generously showed towards Silent Shafiqa and the tenderness and concern she displayed for her condition. She also took charge of Shafiqa's ration of food, handing it to her herself and had it not been for her perseverance in watching over her, this wretched creature would have perished long ago.

Umm Abdel Aziz tried to keep an eye on Silent Shafiqa, especially when she had sudden attacks of nervous convulsions which took her by surprise from time to time. On these occasions the skinny young girl was transformed into a rigid block of wood; sometimes she threw herself on the ground and her unfocused eyes would bulge in a frightening way as she turned her head like a young calf about to be slaughtered, the white froth trickling from her mouth in a thin stream. All the prisoners and warders who came across this spectacle by chance were at a loss as to what to do at which point Umm Abdel Aziz would approach muttering the two Qur'anic formulae followed by the verse, "Say, I take refuge with the Lord of men". She would bend down to the girl who had thrown herself on the floor, and with her mouth close to her right ear, call her to prayer in a beautiful voice. This would be followed by a recitation of some of the ninety-nine names attributed to God which came to her mind. She would ask the Prophet's forgiveness for the girl – Peace be upon Him – and would stay with her until the life returned to her body. Hugging her to her large breast which could have accommodated another besides the tiny Shafiqa, she would hasten to give her a drink of water and soothe her tenderly as the girl's hot tears flowed onto her cheek.

Shafiqa reminded Umm Abdel Aziz of her son who was martyred in the 1973 war, because of their strong physical resemblance, especially her thick arched eyebrows and wide-set eyes and the gap they both had between their front teeth which is meant to bring good luck – although time had already disproved this maxim. The wretched girl's luck had only landed her in prison; as for the apple of Umm Abdel Aziz's eye, his luck had landed him under the ground. Because she did not even know the whereabouts of his grave she was unable to go and visit it and honour him, as a martyr of the Sinai war, by erecting a headstone to immortalize his name. The bitterness and perpetual grief she suffered from being separated from him would never diminish. Following his recognition as a martyr, she received a considerable amount of money in compensation. After selling a pair of gold snakes left over from her wedding jewellery, she was able to add two floors onto her old house, but not before paying the municipal officials to give her the necessary authorization – a violation of the law although not the one which landed her in prison. She was convicted for the money she received from renting out private rooms when the profit she made from her combined building and renting transactions jumped to at least 300%. The exploited people who were renting from her were civil servants on meagre salaries who could only pay their deposit to Hajja Umm Abdel Aziz with great difficulty, after tightening their belts and setting aside the necessary monthly sum from their salary to participate with their colleagues in the self-styled cooperatives or associations. These provided them with the deposit each one had to pay. The civil servants brought a complaint concerning the money Umm Abdel Aziz had extracted from them and the law considered she had committed a serious crime. But this did nothing to help the tenants with their problem which came to a head when the flats were sold off privately instead of being rented out. Umm Abdel Aziz was duly sent to prison, but she did not object because she was given a short sentence. The judge who passed sentence took compassion on her because of her age and the esteem he had for her as the mother of a martyr in the war.

Umm Abdel Aziz was a model prisoner in every sense. She was intelligent, self-possessed, well turned out. She kept a civil tongue and showed consideration for the lowly over the exalted. The prisoners and warders had a certain respect for the kind of offence she had been charged with since, in their view, it was not without distinction and didn't in any way put them off being her friends. Her only fault was her continual snoring which started as soon as her head touched the pillow and sounded like water dripping from a leaking tap. The combined snoring of Umm Ragab and Umm El-Khayr formed a deafening symphony when added to that of Umm Abdel Aziz who slept in the same ward. Apart from this Umm Abdel Aziz commanded a position of respect, especially since many of the inmates had formed the view that she was a pious woman, one of those who had attained spiritual communion with God. She prayed a great deal and fasted every Monday and Thursday, as well as during the month of Ramadan, the six days which follow it, the first of Ragab, the middle of Sha'ban and the first days of the holy months. Likewise she was respected for the obvious blessing that had been bestowed on her and her ability to restore Silent Shafiqa to her former self. She would bend over her right ear to call her to prayer when she was overcome by fits of devilish madness, believed to be no more than severe epileptic fits which had never been treated. As a result of the trust and belief the prisoners as well as the warders placed in Umm Abdel Aziz, she spent hours making amulets for the prisoners, commiserating with them, stroking their heads and reading them verses from the Qur'an to soothe them when they were afflicted by severe headaches which they could not cure with any of the array from Bayer or Swiss Pharma pills which claimed to alleviate pain. The real cause of their problems was the increasing weakness in their eyesight due to lack of vitamin A in the food, as well as the chronic constipation they suffered because of a lack of roughage in the prison meals. The faith which Umm Abdel Aziz inspired grew to such an extent that she was encouraged to start interpreting dreams, usually with a group of prisoners collected around her who considered this activity a kind of delicious scandal. Umm Abdel Aziz's ability to interpret dreams correctly and precisely was established when she told Mahrousa, the warder, that she had a daughter who would soon marry against her wishes. One morning Mahrousa had told her about a dream in which one of her daughters, who was the most beautiful, was eating a large banana. She tried to stop her eating it by convincing her that it was poisonous and might harm her. When the young girl insisted, Mahrousa screamed and cried for help at which point she was awakened by the voice of the *fuul* seller who was calling out in the alley. She awoke from her sleep, terrified, and went to the kitchen to fetch the Istanbuli porcelain bowl which she had got in exchange for some old trousers which belonged to her son, and went out to buy some *fuul*. When she returned home that afternoon at the end of her day's work in the prison, her daughter, who in her opinion was a flighty girl and deserved to have her neck broken, declared that she both desired and intended to marry an electrician.

The strange thing is that, with time, Umm Abdel Aziz, began to really believe in her special powers to remove the veil from dreams. She extended her prayer routine while continuing to recite parts of the Qur'an in addition to the five prescribed prayers and the prayers invoking God. She also recited from the cheap religious booklets handed to her by Mahrousa, who never tired of having her dreams interpreted. Mahrousa bought the books especially for her from the sellers who lined the wall of the Sayyida Zaynab mosque and the wall of the Hussein mosque, may God bless them. But one night, while Umm Abdel Aziz was sitting on her bed singing God's praises with her old rosary made from ambergris, bought from the Khan Al-Khalili souk, she was finally convinced that the veil had been removed from her and the path which led directly to God had opened before her. The pampered prison cat was next to her, purring peacefully, when she felt engulfed by a surge of love and longing to see her only martyred son who had been taken away from her. It affected her so strongly that her heart beat quickened, she felt an abnormal rush of blood to her head and her fingers were no longer able to move the rosary beads easily. At the time there was a terrible racket going on in the ward for the old and weak because of a quarrel which had broken out between Umm Ragab and Lula the hairdresser. A box of matches had gone missing which Lula had accused Umm Ragab of stealing. The din was augmented by voices from other quarters which had joined in to try and settle the dispute. But despite all this distraction, Umm Abdel Aziz actually witnessed, with her own eyes, her dearest elder son, Abdel Aziz, with his beautiful features which greatly resembled those of Silent Shafiqa, coming towards her in his military uniform. Then he sat down next to her on the edge of the bed and stroked the head of the cat which enjoyed it greatly, lifting its head a little for him to scratch its neck and chin which were troubling it because of flea bites. Umm Abdel Aziz even heard his voice with her own ears, which despite her age were sharp enough to hear ants crawling. He asked her gently:

"Do you want anything, Hajja, before I return?"

Barely a second later he disappeared and the bereaved mother had to open and shut her eyes vigorously several times to convince herself that what she had witnessed was real and not a dream. When she felt the place where he had been sitting on the bed and found that it was warm, as if someone had just left, she was convinced it was not a dream and let out a piercing scream, beating her chest with her hands, calling her beloved son. All this commotion caused astonishment in the ward and halted the quarrel between Umm Ragab and Lula, who gave the cat a strong kick with her foot when it jumped down with fright at Umm Abdel Aziz's scream and tripped her up.

After slapping her face and lamenting for some time the grieving mother eventually regained her composure. She was joined by Azima the professional mourner and Umm Ragab, who saw it as a good opportunity to lament her daughter. Hinna expended extraordinary efforts in quietening and calming her, stroking her face with a piece of cotton cloth, soaked in rose water, and wrapping her hair in a different handkerchief to the one she had removed to hold while eulogizing over the moral and various other qualities of her son, now destroyed by treacherous death and swallowed up by the earth. When Umm Abdel Aziz had completely exhausted her strength and emotions and was no longer capable of releasing any more grief, she remained silent and grave-faced, ignoring all questions aimed at discovering what had made her scream and wail in this uncharacteristic way. No one had ever seen her in such a terrible state of collapse and grief before; she had always shown patience and was constantly reading the Qur'an. Even when Hinna asked her a direct question about what had happened, Umm Abdel Aziz chose to keep the secret to herself and hide the matter from everyone. She considered the vision of her dead son, which she had seen with her own eyes, a token of compassion and generosity which God had bestowed upon her and which called for inward thanks, praise and self-restraint.

After asking for protection from Satan, Umm Abdel Aziz stood up and performed the ritual ablution before prayer and prayed extremely devoutly, asking God's pardon for what she had just done because she had not intended to oppose his wishes. She spent the night awake until the stars had disappeared from the sky, reading verses and invocations to comfort her dead son in his grave and to console his relatives in the world of the living.

While all this was going on, Aziza was in her solitary cell, next door to the ward for the weak where these events took place. After hearing the commotion, especially the screaming and the impassioned lamentation, she was gazing at the ceiling and thought again about Umm Abdel Aziz's condition and the bitter torment which she had seldom expressed since she came to prison. As she extinguished her cigarette butt in an old can, which used to contain *qaha* fig jam, she felt a twinge of conscience because she had taken the wrong view over whether to allow this unfortunate old woman to join the golden chariot going to heaven. She got up and went to the window; resting her head between two iron bars she said in low voice, tinged with remorse:

"My mistake! You must go before Shafiqa!"

8

Melody of the Heavenly Ascent

No one ever knew what Aziza the Alexandrian did while she remained alone in her solitary cell for fourteen hours each day – after the door had been locked from the outside at about five in the afternoon until it was opened by the duty warder at seven o'clock the next morning. The prisoners in the ward for the weak next door could hear her footsteps for most of the night as she paced anxiously up and down, rarely stopping. Nothing else could be heard from her cell as she carried on extended conversations with her mother, the murdered husband, herself and those selected to ascend in the magical, golden chariot with wings, taking them to the other beautiful world in the sky. These conversations remained an everlasting secret to all except the spiders on the ceiling of her cell which shared her nightly vigil, hunting for any available small insects, dazzled by the light coming from the ward at night. The crickets in the field also kept this solitary woman company, sending friendly greetings to her as she sat sipping her imaginary wine. The sound of their chirping reached the cell through the open window from their habitat in the fields by the river bank, not far from the prison.

Aziza was allowed to stay in the women's prison for many years instead of being moved to the psychiatric hospital because the doctors were mystified by her condition and could find no evidence to justify placing her amongst the band of those who had lost their reason and strayed from the commonly accepted boundaries of the human herd. As to the rare minor outbursts which escaped from her during her time in prison, the investigation took the view that if the angels themselves had been exposed to these conditions they would have borne evil Satanic fangs and sharp nails to oppose those who sought to triumph over them and provoke them. As far as provocative behaviour was concerned, Aziza usually contented herself with a small bite, like the one she gave Lula the hairdresser because she was insolent, or with pulling someone's hair or perhaps hitting her adversary on the chest and nose as she did once with the troublesome warder. This warder had a pale gloomy face, like one of the thieves of death who dig up graves and had now made Jamalat the target of her evil doings, picking on her for the slightest thing because the girl had once refused to wash her clothes for her after burning her hand with hot oil when she was frying potatoes. Apart from minor incidents like this Aziza did nothing else which attracted attention or pointed to her madness except perhaps for the way she talked to herself – sometimes in the presence of others – which is something which happens to nearly everyone. The only difference was that Aziza did it in an audible voice and gossiped about whatever and whoever she liked, irrespective of whether it was true or not or whether it was appropriate. She called a spade a spade, which was precisely what people often wanted to do but held back through cowardice.

Aziza's condition and the audible conversations she had with herself in the prison courtyard or in the long corridor which her cell and others overlooked, never caused anxiety to anyone. This included the prison administration itself whose decision to place her in the solitary cell was a precaution against incidents which could give rise to unneccessary problems.

When she was in her cell Aziza often thought about the notion of prison as a system of punishment which society had collectively chosen and she realized that the idea behind punishment, which made one person an example for others, could not be applied in her case.

She could never be an example to anyone else since her life had been unique – a life no other woman could have experienced. Only a mermaid, which can sink itself far, far into the depths of the sea without fear or dread, would be able to endure such a life, because she knows the secrets hidden in the sea and knows about the raging waves just as Aziza knew about the sea of passion and knew its horrors and pains. Besides, Aziza had not killed out of a desire for murder or for revenge, nor was she motivated by anger and hatred. She killed for the sake of preserving her unique passionate love and she only lived so that its tree should for ever mature and flourish. The person she killed was another person who resembled him. She had decided to get rid of him after he had taken on the guise of her mother's husband and only so that she could protect what she had cherished throughout her life. He stole the eternal flame of her passionate love and uprooted the tree of life from its very depths.

Not for one moment did Aziza regret carrying out the murder. Nor did she regret burning the house by pouring kerosene in every corner which had witnessed a single detail of their love and moment of intense passion. These were secrets known only to this house, set in the heart of its magnificent garden, the house which resounded with a secret life of the kind unexperienced by anyone before. Equally she never regretted leading a life like a pious Sufi, praying in the niche of her mad passion. However, there was one thing she did bitterly regret: that she allowed her worshipped lover to attach himself to another and that he should have reached the point of marriage to the one he loved. Aziza bit her fingers with regret because she had allowed the matter to start like a little abrasion and that the purity of her beautiful love had become soiled. She had failed to stop the saga in its early stages; she had lacked the courage to do what she did later, the moment her heart sank in fear and terror as she caught the look her chosen idol gave Nadira – the look she never imagined he would direct to anyone but her. From that moment she felt that the love and passion filling her heart no longer belonged to her and that she must act without further delay; she could not bet on the hope that what had taken place was only a passing summer cloud which would go of its own accord without flooding the secret little island of love whose delights she had feasted on, where she had lived and where she had so often wished she could remain for all eternity.

Many a night Aziza spent hours conversing with the lover she thought was eternally hers, all the while believing she had been created only to love him and had lived only because the breath of his soul was coursing through her blood making her a unique woman, devoted to this venerated loved one. She wanted him to see her in a state of constantly renewed freshness as if she were a beautiful phoenix which would never die nor quench its thirst from the water of life. Many a time would she chat with him during her nights, imagining sweet wine when she was only intoxicated by the memories of her life which flowed out of her, from behind the high prison walls, far from her beloved city by the sea. Frequently a longing surfaced for her mother, her friend and soul-mate, partner of the same body and companion of days past who had been carried away by time. She was the fresh flower of the house who always blessed the support and kindness between her husband and daughter and nurtured the tree of her love through the support of her own compassion and love. She never tried to listen or use her other senses to detect what her eyes failed to distinguish – the silent cries which revealed the passionate relationship between her beloved husband and her only little girl, always preoccupied with her passion in that old house which witnessed both moments of birth and painful moments of death.

As Aziza sat on her own in her cell she decided that her mother must have discovered the truth about the relationship between her daughter and husband and approved of it, preferring to keep silent for many reasons. Perhaps she had considered it a source of happiness for the treasure of her heart and the light of her life, through which she, who was denied the light in her eyes, could see. She had been quite happy for them to go out together on the many days and nights they spent having fun and staying up late. It was she who had encouraged her husband to accompany her daughter to the capital which was called the 'Mother of the World' and to show her around. What was more she had urged her daughter to care for him and look after his interests, making her personally responsible for laying out his clothes when he was going out and preparing his food for him when he stayed home for the evening; she had suckled her with his love and passion just as she had suckled her with the milk from her breast and perhaps she had known that this sympathy and kindness could grow and mature into what was beyond . . . to the limits of passion and love.

However what caused Aziza pain and anxiety, and even made her feel ashamed, was that she never would have been so accommodating to her mother if she had been in her place nor would she have allowed her daughter to be her husband's lover and flirt with the man that she loved passionately and was also married to. Her feelings of shame and anxiety stemmed from self-recrimination over her cruelty and, more important still, her extreme ingratitude towards this kind mother who had been tolerant, generous-hearted and never for a moment ceased to surround her with love and affection.

As these painful thoughts passed through Aziza's mind, an uncontrollable anger took hold of her . . . anger which was turned against herself because she had never been a dutiful daughter. She had been ungrateful and selfish, taking what she would deny her mother who was solely responsible for introducing her to the man she loved so much, with whom she experienced such beautiful times. Aziza felt a violent pain rage within her which shook her very being, invading her tormented spirit in which the owl and wind had long set up their lamenting moan. She suddenly stood up and paced up and down between the four high walls. As her pain reached a climax she went to the window, touched the rusty iron bars and shook them as if all her pain and anger were concentrated in the grip of her hand. It was as if she wanted to smash them and push herself through to reach outside, far away, high up in the sky. It was then that the prisoners in the ward for the weak heard a sound coming from Aziza's room next door, which they thought was the cats who kept jumping through the window into her cell. Umm Abdel Aziz believed that Aziza was in league with the Jinn which came to her at night in the form of cats because, if these cats had been like the other stray cats which slipped into the wards at night to steal food, regardless of who they belonged to, Aziza would have chased them away. When Umm Abdel Aziz discussed the matter of these nocturnal cats with Aziza one morning, she categorically denied that any cats visited her during the night. The elderly Hajja, who believed that the veil of God's mysterious world had been lifted before her in prison, wanted to glean some information on this subject from Aziza. She was keen to enlarge her knowledge of the unknown and to sanctify it for the purpose of her new activity which had proved successful through her experience in prison and which she decided to pursue and refine after she left to lead a normal life.

Aziza was unable to break the bars and hurt her hands so much that she had no energy left to push away this barrier impeding the release of her torment and the ascent to where she wanted to go. She was forced to return to her mattress on the floor, dragging her body, drained through all the suffering. She sat, a heap of humanity, destroyed by life and mocked by time, her grey hair and the finely engraved lines around her eyes had lost the lustre of life leaving a sleepy, arrogant look, a faint reminder of what she used to look like in the past. As soon as she had thrown herself onto the thin sponge mattress, she lit another cigarette and drank a glass of her 'wine' in quick gulps to repress the burning pain and to concentrate her thoughts sufficiently to ensure that the golden chariot would make the ascent to heaven in the highest state of readiness.

Aziza wanted the passengers of her golden chariot to look as beautiful as humanly possible for their ascent from earth to heaven. She believed that this was the minumum required and befitted those chosen. For that reason she spent long nights discussing with Sonia the Armenian, formerly the most renowned dressmaker in Alexandria, who had often made the most beautiful garments for Aziza and her mother according to the latest fashion. Aziza invited Sonia from France where she had recently emigrated to join her sons who had opened a Middle Eastern restaurant there. She discussed every little detail with Sonia concerning the kind of cloth, the colour and the suitability of all kinds of garments which she would be making for her and the friends chosen to accompany her on the golden chariot. Then she saw each of the prisoners who would be joining the chariot in turn, so that she could take their measurements and decide on the most suitable style for them. Throughout this procedure, she consulted Zaynab Mansur who sat next to her and, with the benefit of her fine aristocratic taste, supervised every detail concerning the dresses, selecting the most magnificent cloth in glorious colours of the best taste to make them look like angels, no less beautiful and splendid than the angels in the sky. They were to be long, full-waisted dresses made from crêpe de chine, fine chiffon, shantung silk and duchesse satin, lace and tulle, embroidered with gold and silver thread and sequins, sparkling with all the colours of the rainbow, just like the necks of the local pigeons, fit to meet the angels in. For each of them Aziza choose golden crowns set with jewels and precious stones which were breathtakingly magical. She wanted these crowns to resemble the crown Farida wore on the night of her marriage to King Farouk. Aziza detested him because he divorced Farida and married Nariman, but God, who always puts things right, toppled him from his throne a short time after when the Revolution broke out and he left the country disgraced, abandoning everything. Meanwhile the picture of Farida, in her splendid long wedding dress and her crown on her head, hung on the wall next to Aziza's bed. She had been in the habit of feasting her eyes on it from time to time until one particularly violent day, one of the days when the *Nuwwa* wind blows in from the sea, the window, which had no secure catch, was blown wide open and the picture flew away. All trace of the picture was lost, washed away by the rain which poured down on it in the garden.

As to the shoes, they would match the clothes perfectly. Aziza chose black satin or fine leather mixed with a few bits of drawn thread work and smooth chamois velvet. All of them would have plain heels, not very high, except for Hinna's which would be seven centimetres high. Azima, the female mourner, would have completely flat shoes but they would be embroidered with beautiful silver thread and she would make her sit at the end of the chariot so as not to block the view of those sitting in front of her. She would arrange this tactfully without hurting her feelings as people had done in the past. Azima had told her one day, in a sad tone, that because she was so tall she was made to clean the ceilings in her father's house in order to save him buying one of the long, wooden-handled brushes used for this purpose. And that one of their neighbours would send her young daughter to fetch Azima so that she could get something down from one of the high old cupboards which she could not reach herself. This made Azima extremely annoyed because she hated anything which reminded her of her unusual height.

Aziza decided to put Adli, the hairdresser, in charge of the women's hair because he was an artist who specialized in dressing women's hair and whose golden fingers would be able to transform their heads into something resembling the magic mermaids. He was the hairdresser from her city who had so often skilfully arranged her hair, always in ways which won the admiration of her lover and dazzled him because he made her look even more beautiful and enchanting. Aziza decided, after thinking extremely hard, to include the tormented prison cat amongst the passengers as well as another black cat which she often saw around the prison. It sometimes sat next to the prison cat in the corridor, part of which Aziza could see from the other window in her room. She noticed how they meowed together in utter contentment, and never fought with each other, even over the food which was thrown to them during the night.

Despite all the planning Aziza did to ensure that the ascent should be as well prepared as possible, there were some minor obstacles to overcome. There was the problem of Mahrousa, the warder, who loathed Umm Ragab because she spied on the prisoners for the prison authorities. This role caused Mahrousa considerable anguish; she was accused of colluding with some of the prisoners although, as far as she was concerned, she was simply helping them out of kindness. On one occasion, Umm El-Khayr made a life-size rag doll for Aida, the Saïdi girl, so that she could hug it when she went to sleep as if it were her little boy but Umm Ragab stole it. When Mahrousa reproached her for this, she took revenge on her and informed the prison authorities that Mahrousa had allowed Jamalat to leave her own ward and spend a night with Huda in the scabies ward. Huda had tempted her with an invitation to an evening of singing and dancing, celebrating the release of a prisoner due to take place the following day. The order for her release had been given because the charge of having two husbands could not be substantiated. The court discovered that her first husband, who had left the country seven years ago, had died and that during his absence she had neither seen nor heard anything of him. She had moved to a town in the Saïd and married a pedlar selling molasses, with whom she had three children, but the mother of her first husband took legal action against her to try and land her in prison.

Silent Shafiqa posed another problem for Aziza. Most of the prisoners objected to her presence, despite feeling sympathy for her, because she was so filthy and insisted on wearing the bare minimum of clothing, even in the depths of winter, resisting all attempts made to provide her with something to cover her body. But Aziza was banking on their accepting her and rejoicing with her after she had been bathed; her body would be well scrubbed with a loofah and her heels rubbed with a pumice stone until they became as smooth as the satin of her rose-coloured dress with its slightly décolleté neckline and full skirt, gathered in at the waist and made with Sonia's expertise. Then Adli the hairdresser would comb her beautiful soft hair and arrange it in an amazing plait at the back, fixed by a large hairpin made of ivory and studded with diamonds. By this time she would be a totally different woman, bearing no resemblance to the filthy dispirited girl that she was now. Perhaps she might even resemble the beautiful Shadia in the film, with the song called "Search and you will find", which Aziza had seen in the Metro cinema in Alexandria one day with her lover. Her mother had urged him to take her out and cheer her up a little after she had spent ten days in bed with a fever from severe inflammation of the colon which at first the doctors thought might have been typhoid. On that day he had held her hand in the dark and planted occasional kisses on her cheek.

Aziza was sometimes kept awake at night, terrified by the thought that the prison governor himself might notice the chariot and try to stop it when he realized it was going to ascend to that beautiful place in heaven where there is grace and favour, everlasting, supreme happiness and true, deep love between human beings and where they would not be kept awake by continual quarrels and strife. Aziza pondered at length over this problem and how to confront it should it really occur. Accordingly, she decided that take-off would be at night when the governor would not be in the prison and the operation could proceed with secrecy, calm and speed. She would beg the horses not to attract attention to the chariot by neighing in their lovely way or making the magical sound from flapping their powerful golden wings until the whistle was blown. She would then be able to rouse the sleeping prisoners and get them onto the chariot. The order would be given to everyone who had been chosen for the ascent to proceed quickly, carefully, and with calm before the prison governor arrived, discovered the affair and tried to ascend with it, only complicating matters.

This fear kept Aziza awake all night after she had stopped thinking about her lover, her mother and the passengers of the chariot ascending to heaven. Her insomnia drove sleep from her eyes so that she was awake to hear the cock crow and the dawn call to prayer on the day before the last night of her life. That night she recalled as many memories as possible which had remained her close companions for all those long and desolate nights in prison and she made all the final arrangements for the ascent of the golden chariot to the heaven. But first she called her selected passengers, one by one, secretly in a voice only audible to her, and dressed each one in her own magnificent tailor-made outfit. She instructed Adli, the hairdresser, to arrange their hair and adorn their heads to make them look as beautiful as possible. At this point the preparations for the ascent, which she had planned down to the last detail in her imagination, were now complete. Aziza wore her long black velvet dress with long sleeves and a bodice made of lace covered with little diamonds, sparkling with all the colours of the rainbow in the shape of beautiful flowers. Then her hair was arranged in her favourite way, which Adli was so expert at doing; on this occasion he did it to perfection, better than any other time. He gathered it and rolled it at the nape of her neck, tying it in a beautiful black satin bow with a little pearl attached to it. Only after she had inspected all the women one by one, and was sure that their attire was everything that it should be – that they were as beautiful and enchanting as possible – did she allow them to mount the chariot. Aziza carried the prison cat, Mishmisha, under her arm, having placed a dark brown velvet collar with a little silver bell around its neck, while her black friend was carried by the peasant, Umm El-Khayr who was as pleased as punch, as if she had stumbled over some treasure. After Aziza had tied a red silk ribbon round its neck, not forgetting to hang a little bell on its collar, the cat looked beautiful and glossy in her shining black coat. When each one had taken her place on the chariot, Aziza signalled to the heavenly band, engaged for the ascent to heaven, to strike up the glorious music which made her tremble with emotion. She had instructed them to play the same tune, engraved in her memory since the time she first heard it played by one of the military bands at the music pavilion in the beautiful Antoniades Gardens, the day the

British Evacuation was celebrated. No one played tunes there anymore, perhaps because the time for celebrating the Evacuation had passed.

Before the dignified ceremony of the heavenly ascent there was a splendid dinner, better than anything you would get in a five star hotel, and a dance which equalled the wonderful dancing Aziza had done with her lover on the floors of the superb city nightclubs at Christmas and on New Year's Eve. Aziza gave a long, farewell look, tinged with scorn, at the whole inhuman world of that fearful prison, the building and its administration, its warders and food, the sleeping quarters and clothes, then she ordered the doors to be locked and gave the signal for take-off. The beautiful, powerful white horses spread out their splendid golden wings like sails of legendary ships about to plough through the billowing waves.

Aziza was surprised when suddenly, and quite inexplicably, the prison governor and the warders, whom she had always hated, arrived in front of the chariot and obstructed it as they climbed on.

At that moment, alone in her cell, Aziza's blood pressure rose dramatically until one clot after another formed in her brain. The brain raced on over times past, the life which had crept along the alleyways of fate and the years of joy and sadness she had experienced, until the very end. Not a solitary star looked down on Aziza as she lost consciousness for the last time and began the final struggle with death. She saw her chosen women rushing to get down from the chariot, jostling with those trying to seize and board it. Once the women had succeeded in repelling them, hurling them beneath the horses' hooves, Aziza struggled to raise her hand for take-off and the horses began to flap their wings in readiness for the ascent.

Aziza's heart began to beat at an alarming rate but she held onto her last breath of life until she was convinced that the women were safely back in the chariot and the windows and doors securely locked. Only then could the white horses lift their hooves and start to fly, with their golden wings, up to heaven.